"MYSTICAL MAGPIES & MYTHOLOGY"

THE TWINS DESTINY BEGINS

THE TWINS DESTINY BEGINS

Alan Principal

© Alan Principal, 2014

Published by Alan Principal

Intellectual Property & Copyright © Alan Principal 2010

First paperback edition printed 2014 in the United Kingdom

This novel is a work of fiction. Names and characters are the product of the author's imagination or historical facts or folklore used with no offensive or slanderous intent. The publisher and author assume no responsibility for errors or omission from the date of printing.

A CIP catalogue record for this book is available from the British Library.

ISBN 978-0-9930139-0-4

Book layout and cover design by Clare Brayshaw

Cover image © Konradbak I Dreamstime.com

Prepared, printed and distributed by:

York Publishing Services Ltd
64 Hallfield Road
Layerthorpe
York YO31 7ZQ

Tel: 01904 431213

Website: www.yps-publishing.co.uk

About the author

Alan is a proud Yorkshireman. He was born, brought up and educated in Doncaster where he still lives with his loving wife Sylvia. His ability as a creative writer was completely missed by his teacher, who wrongly and severely punished him. His 'crime' (for homework at the age of 10) – writing a beautiful poem about the harvest. She thought he'd copied it from a book. Sadly  he didn't resume creatively using his pen until he finished his 3 year service in the Aerial Photo Intelligence section of the Royal Air Force.

His work roles, which eventually steered him to some serious yet pleasant writing, have included teaching and helping thousands of people to drive, training, lecturing, features in the local press, FE teaching, submission writing and a wide range of vocational programme guides for NVQ's to level 4. In 1991 he almost managed to attract the Royal Armouries to a Doncaster site.

Since virtually retiring, he has enjoyed writing quizzes for the company he set up in 1994. In his role as Quizmaster he uses his birth name as he did in his previous involvements.

During the last few years, he has enjoyed writing a kaleidoscope of poetry of both serious and humorous rhymes – a book will probably surface in 2015.

But his greatest authorial love has been penning a series of four exciting and mystical, gripping action packed 'crossover' adventure stories, particularly suitable for those aged 10-20 but good armchair or bedtime reading for all family members who are 'young at heart' aged 10 to 100.

The twins featured with their parents in the first of the four captivating stories 'The Twins Destiny Begins' are 15 years old. In book 2 – 'Retribution' they reach 17, and are 20 in the third and fourth of the sequential stories.

Dedication

I dedicate this book to my wonderful and loving wife Sylvia, without whom the story would never have been told.

My grateful thanks also go to our good friend Patsy Daniels, who patiently typed so well from my sometimes scribbled nots and did such an excellent job helping me with proofreading.

Thank you Ladies

Alan

The Magpies Poem

One for sorrow
Two for joy
Three for a girl
Four for a boy
Five for silver
Six for gold
Seven for a story never to be told
… until now!!!

Contents

Chapter One

A NIGHTMARE JOURNEY

The exciting and magical adventure began on a warm evening in June on the eve of the mystical, sometimes magical Summer Solstice, as two dark shadowy figures slowly and menacingly drifted between the trees on the edge of Bill's garden. Bill Knight, an athletically built martial arts expert, his black hair cut in a military style, was preparing to drive his attractive wife Sylvia to the maternity hospital, as the twins she was expecting, mythologically very special twins, were due to be born. Bill had been an unarmed combat instructor at an RAF Camp in Castershire when he and Sylvia met. Wanting to see more of him, Sylvia joined the martial arts classes Bill ran two nights a week, and surprisingly quickly became the proud owner of a black belt. They were so perfectly suited, for them to marry when they were twenty one seemed as though it had simply been their destiny; and so it was. Bill and Sylvia becoming man and wife was an important part of a centuries old mythological, supernatural plan.

After Bill left the Air Force, they set up home on the outskirts of Oxtown where they established a popular gym called 'Bill Knight's Seven Magpies Martial Arts Studio', both of them teaching a wide range of martial arts disciplines. Now however, Sylvia's labour contractions were happening at shorter intervals and she was beginning to feel rather uncomfortable. It was time to get into their car and drive to the hospital. They were particularly proud of the appearance of their black car displaying their magpie business logo on the driver and front passenger doors, as the magpie images in their emblem represented seven very special magical magpies which meant a lot to them – but more about them later.

Sylvia looked very feminine and very pregnant in her sky blue multi-flowered maternity dress. The dress also showed off her sun tan and ash blond almost white hair, which, just like Bill's black hair, has a supernaturally significant meaning in their story. 'You look blooming lovely,' Bill said as he helped his wife to carefully fit her seat belt after putting her black carry-all bag containing her personal things into the car. As Bill closed the car door he glanced back at the house, the front of which was illuminated by a pair of old-fashioned street lamps positioned either side of the garage doors. It was then he spotted the unwelcome shadowy figures drift across the lawn and seemingly melt into the shadows of the conifers.

Having caught sight of the unwelcome apparitions, Bill's face turned grim and his body tensed as he tightly clenched his fists in anger. He knew such fiendish figures could only mean one thing. **Trouble!** But they had to leave. Sylvia needed to get to the hospital to give birth to their twins.

Understandably groaning, Sylvia took a deep breath and placed her hands on her ample sized stomach as Bill walked round to the driver's side of the car. 'They're here, or at least two of them are,' Bill remarked as he fastened his seat belt. 'I've just spotted a couple of them gliding across the front lawn. We'd better lock the car doors,' and did so as he said it. 'Just to be on the safe side, Sylv', you never know. The last thing we want would be for them to be able to get into the car if for some reason we had to stop.'

'But we shouldn't be surprised they're here though, Bill, should we?' Sylvia said. 'We know how important our twins are. They bring mythology right up to date, and we know the evil Other World also knows about them. This special event, the birth of our twins and what they are destined to become, has been on the cards for centuries. So we had expected some kind of negativity. Sadly, we know what they don't want is for our twins to be born or survive. Let's hope the Gods of the Terrestrial Light who created the plan all those years ago can help us.'

Bill, having wasted no time driving away from the house and the potential danger, headed for the hospital. Glancing at Sylvia he said, 'Yes, love, you're right, I know we've got to expect something, but the trouble is....... what? Both of us were twins, but sadly your brother and my sister mysteriously died shortly after being born, and both our families felt sure it was **them** from the Other World who were responsible. It just doesn't seem fair.

'But one thing we do know is our twins on their fifteenth birthday in Castershire are destined to become the central part of a very special mythological event of mammoth proportions. And there are only two things we can do about that: nothing and damn all! So let's hope we don't have any problems en route or at the hospital tonight.'

At that moment Bill's conversation was terrifyingly abruptly halted by a mind-blowing loud explosive noise as their car's windscreen shattered to look like frosted glass. He then needed to grip tighter on to the steering wheel as he felt the nearside front tyre blow, making the steering extremely difficult. He knew from his specialist driver training that the car could skew round and possibly flip over; but by braking smoothly he was able to safely stop.

Sylvia in her sensitive condition couldn't help shrieking out when the car bumped up and on to the grass verge before stopping. Bill reached over to take hold of her hand asking, 'Are you all right, love?'

'Yes, thankfully I am,' she replied sounding rather shaken, 'but what the hell was it, Bill? What happened?'

'The windscreen shattered and the front nearside tyre blew-out,' Bill replied, 'but I'm glad for all our sakes your safety airbag didn't blow out and crush the twins. Perhaps that's what they were hoping would happen.'

'So you think it was **them**?' Sylvia tensely remarked.

'Yes, love, I do. I can't think of any other reason why both things would have happened at the same time, but you need to get to the hospital. I'd better phone for an ambulance.' And using his mobile phone he did, after suggesting to Sylvia, 'You had better keep your door locked, love, until the ambulance arrives, just in case we have unwelcome visitors.'

He gave their location and Sylvia's condition to the telephonist and returned his phone to his shirt pocket. Sylvia was now experiencing even stronger labour pains and wishing it was Bill who was expecting their twins, not her.

'They shouldn't be long now, love,' Bill said, again holding her hand. Sylvia nodded and tried to smile back as an ambulance with its emergency lights flashing came round the bend. 'My god,' Bill went on to say, 'that was quick. They must have been returning from somewhere!'

The ambulance pulled up just ahead of where their car had stopped on the grass verge, and two men wearing green uniforms got out.

'What the hell happened?' questioned the driver.

'What the hell indeed,' Bill replied, somewhat perturbed by the driver's brusque attitude

'Perhaps you hit an owl or something,' said the second man, shooting a sidelong glance at his partner as he helped

Bill to support Sylvia as she stepped out of the car on to the grass.

The driver seemed to calm down a little and it was as though he had anticipated Bill's question, for as he opened the rear door of the ambulance he said, 'It was lucky for you we were in the area. We had been called out to a false alarm and had just started back when we received the message. That was why we were able to get here so quickly...... Don't worry ......It won't be long now!'

Bill made sure their car was securely locked before climbing into the ambulance and was again holding his wife's hand as the ambulance doors closed. But then, with alarm on his face, he gripped Sylvia's hand tighter as he heard the lock snap into place after the doors were shut. For some reason, which he didn't like one bit, they had been locked in!

Being locked in the back of the ambulance prevented either of them from witnessing the dull red glow that had appeared in the eyes of both men as they climbed back into their seats.

'No, it won't be long now,' the driver sarcastically repeated giving a hideous laugh. 'We should see the end of the lot of them in just a minute or two. None of them will ever get to Castershire after tonight's short journey.'

'Yes,' his mate said, grinning with what looked like a caved-in toothless mouth, 'we'll get all four of them at the same time.' Then referring to the chief goblin he said, 'King Offalmire will be really pleased with us, especially as it means we've got all of them.'

The driver nodded and said, 'He won't want to hurt you this time like he did when he gave you an important job and you failed to do it.'

'Yes,' grunted his mate, 'Offalmire is totally evil. He pulled out all my teeth without giving me any painkillers. It was terrible! Just hating him is not enough!'

The ambulance was now being driven erratically, weaving from one side of the road to the other. On one bend it only just missed hitting some trees, and Bill was having difficulty holding his wife on the stretcher bed on which they were seated. At one point a cyclist had to jump for his life to avoid being hit by the ambulance as it wildly careered off into the night.

Suddenly it screeched to a stop; but as both Sylvia and Bill were now seated up against the bulkhead of the ambulance, they weren't thrown forward so were not hurt. The ambulance's engine and its flashing lights were then turned off.

As one of the side windows was slightly open, it enabled Bill to look out. Just as he did, a loud clanging noise started and some different lights began to flash which brought a sickening mixed feeling of both terror and anger to Bill's whole being.

'**What the hell's that?**' shrieked Sylvia in a panicked voice as Bill dropped to his knees in front of her, this time grabbing hold of both her hands.

'They've stopped the ambulance halfway across a ruddy level crossing,' he angrily snarled.

Then, thinking quickly said, 'We were both twins, and twinning might work for us and our special twins, it's got to! In fact, it's our only hope, so let's try it!' Gripping his wife's hands even tighter he continued, 'I love you, Sylv'.'

'And I love you too,' she replied. Then, having crossed their clenched hands they looked up, and as if they had rehearsed it, together loudly said, '**Please, Gods of the Terrestrial Light, please help us and your Terrestrial Twins!**'

The two ambulance men were just about to get out of the ambulance when their door locks clicked into place preventing their doors from opening. 'Aw hell, no!' the driver exclaimed.

In the same split second, a blinding beam of white and pale blue shimmering light suddenly engulfed all of the ambulance. Then, as quickly as it had arrived, the light was gone.

Real fear then spread across the faces of both men, their eyes flashing, changing from dull to bright red and back again as they desperately tried but failed to open their doors. Looking to their right, they both screamed, 'NO! NO! NOT US!' in frightened anticipation of what was about to happen. In the same blink of an eye, a ghost train appeared, for that's what it was, with its huge evil-toothed mouth now gaping wide open. It made everything shake as it roared out of the darkness and flashed through the level crossing where the ambulance was standing, gobbling it up with one snap of its jaws. The train then vanished in a puff of orange and purple smoke......

Once more the night became still, except for the hoot of an owl and, strangely, the sight of four magpies sitting on one barrier of the crossing and three sitting on the other. And oddly enough, they were all giggling, really giggling.....But what had happened to Sylvia and Bill.....?

Chapter Two

TWO ENTITIES SNEAK IN

As the supernatural light faded from around them, Sylvia and Bill were amazed to find themselves standing in a corner at the side of the hospital close to the Maternity Unit entrance.

In an excited voice Bill said, 'We did it love, we did it! It worked! The twinning, it thankfully worked for us!'

Sylvia wanted to be excited about it too, but the pain she was now experiencing as their twins became even more active, made her think of other things. Bill, carefully supporting her, began slowly walking towards the entrance.

A nurse having spotted them ran out accompanied by a porter pushing a wheelchair, and Sylvia, relieved, gladly sat in it.

'Good evening,' the porter pleasantly said, 'I'm Frank, but the important one here is Nurse Joyce.'

The nurse smiled and said, 'Hello!' Then went on to say, 'I think we'd better take you to the preparation room first, you can give me your details when we've got you settled. I'll pass them to reception later. First of all we need to make you comfortable.'

Bill was about to again take hold of his wife's hand, but Sylvia pulled hers away to hold her stomach and through wincing teeth said, 'Aw, Bill, I think these two are already practising their martial arts kicks.'

They arrived at the preparation room and Bill gave Sylvia's details to Nurse Joyce. 'Good luck,' Frank said and left.

The nurse, having called up Sylvia's name and notes on the computer, printed a name tag for Sylvia's wrist. She then telephoned for the duty doctor as Sylvia had asked for a pain killing injection to help her with the twins' births.

Apparently the twins had extraordinarily and uniquely – the consultant had actually said 'magically'– developed in Sylvia's womb connected together, and both were sharing the same blood supply. They had also incredibly and mysteriously 'twinned', grasping each other's hands, which they were still doing on the last scan picture of Sylvia's stomach. The type of birth it was to be was now up to the twins. If they released their twinning grip, it would probably be a normal one. If not, a cesarean.

After Sylvia had received the injection, the porter returned to push her in the wheelchair up the corridor to a delivery room. He then left taking the wheelchair with him.

However, because a light bulb had blown, the light outside the hospital entrance was much dimmer than normal. As a result, none of them had noticed the two small dark creatures which had craftily sneaked a ride into the hospital in the base of the wheelchair, having climbed into it when Sylvia was being wheeled in. Once the delivery room was reached, the entities again took advantage of everyone concentrating on Sylvia to slip out of the chair unnoticed. Having cleverly scuttled into the shadows, they hid on the room's windowsill behind the curtain.

Bill was helping Nurse Joyce to make his wife comfortable on the delivery bed as they now felt it would probably be a normal birth, when another nurse wearing a dark blue uniform came into the room. She was a short, chubby, grey haired lady with a big beaming smile on her face. 'Hello and welcome,' she said. 'I'm Sister Pat Gentley.' Bill flashed a quick smiling glance at his wife. But Sister Pat, anticipating through experience, guessed what he was thinking, pleasantly smiled and said, 'No, you can't.' Bill, slightly embarrassed, just shrugged his shoulders and nervously grinned. However, Sylvia was now past the point of joking, as the twins were extremely active and their births' seemed imminent.

So this is it, Bill thought to himself. I hope there aren't going to be any more attempts on Sylvia's or the twins' lives. These two caring nurses are looking after her and the birth of our twins, but they have no idea how special and fundamentally important they are, or the significance of their births.

But being their parents, both Bill and Sylvia did appreciate the enormity of the twins' births. They were fully aware of what was going to happen to them. They knew that at the hour of midnight on their fifteenth birthday, in the mystical time of the Summer Solstice, the twins' lives would totally change. In a supernatural and very special ceremony at a magical ancient megalith in Castershire, and as part of a mythological plan created centuries ago by the Gods of the Terrestrial Light, their twins would become the Terrestrial Twins.

It had been planned for the twins to be blessed with powers and unique supernatural abilities, both as individuals and as twins, and especially through twinning, with the intention of enabling them to become the only humans who might be capable of defeating all sorts of evil entities from the Other World. It was feared that the leader of the Other World, the evil King Offalmire, in fifteen years' time would gain enough power and energy to be able to steal the 'Thirteen Treasures of Britain'. Thirteen magical items which had been hidden and supernaturally sealed in an invisible crystal tower by Merlin many centuries ago. Offalmire had to be prevented from doing this, whatever the cost. For if he was ever able to get his claw-like hands on the supernatural and magical items, he would be able to develop the power to destroy all that is good in Britain as we know it. Stopping him was to be the first assignment of the twins' planned destiny, and that was why his henchmen, mainly Offalmire's entities, various sorts of goblins, were doing their best to make sure the 'Terrestrial Twins' did not arrive or survive.

Both nurses, Pat and Joyce, were busy looking after Sylvia, who, as the twins had released each other's hands, was now having a natural birth. It was while the birth was in progress that Bill became alarmed and angry. He had spotted the two small dark shapes menacingly glide from behind the window curtain and drift down into the room. They then scurried round to and hid behind the monitoring cabinet and gas and air bottles on the far side of the bed... Two of Offalmire's goblins had sneaked in! Sylvia and the twins' safety were yet again being threatened!

From the activity round his wife's bed it appeared their first twin was now being born. As his wife was having problems, Sister Pat asked Bill to switch on the gas and air mask to help Sylvia with the births. Bill had learned how to do this in ante-natal classes, just in case help was needed.

Not wishing to alert the nurses to the presence of the entities, nor the goblins of him, Bill quietly and stealthily crept close to the cabinet and the gas and air bottles. After switching them on, he peered down to look at the unwelcome intruders. The heads of the two Offalmire goblins had the appearance of the tops of ink cap toadstools. Their ears, even more oddly, were like split spiky horse chestnut cases, and they both had their knobbly fingers firmly rammed into them in an attempt to reduce the sound of Sylvia's birth pains. As their eyes were also tightly closed to avoid the bright light that was helping the nurses to see what was happening, neither of the goblins had heard or seen Bill approach their hiding place. Bill shuddered, having seen that both entities had the disgusting goblin characteristic of having candle-like streams of slimy snot running down from their noses.

Seeing the nurses were totally occupied with his wife, Bill quickly grabbed both goblins by their scrawny necks and, by treading on the feet of the pair of them, he was able to pull them up and stretch their necks until their dull red eyes bulged. Then, with super quick movements of his hands and arms, he tied the horrible little creatures' necks into an uncomfortable knot.

Having already noticed there was a large spare pillow propped behind the cabinet, Bill removed the pillowcase, realizing it made an ideal container into which he could put the unwelcome visitors. He then, after firstly wiping his hands on it, rather roughly stuffed the silently squirming goblins into the pillowcase, then rather angrily rammed it down out of sight behind the gas and air bottles.

At that moment, Pat proudly announced, 'Look! You have a beautiful daughter,' and lifted their first baby for them both to see before passing her to Joyce.

Bill was back at his wife's side now to squeeze her right hand as she put down the mask, attempting a smile. 'She looks gorgeous, love, just like you!' he said.

Sylvia's smile was short-lived and she lifted and returned the mask to her face as she again experienced more pangs of labour. Their son was now being born.

Bill had never felt so totally helpless. Here was his wife in agony, and he could do no more than hold her hand. He hoped it was enough.

It was at that moment that Pat, speaking very loudly, said..... **'Well I never!** Never in all my years as a midwife have I ever experienced anything like it!'

Bill suddenly felt sick. Had they, those from the Other World managed to do something evil, and he squeezed his wife's hand.

But Pat then went on to say, and in a much calmer and happier voice, 'You now not only have a handsome son as well as a lovely daughter,' she paused before lifting him, 'but they are both images of you two. Your daughter's hair is white and your son's hair is black, and each of them is holding their own hands as they can't as yet reach each other. What a clever couple you are. None of the other twins I've brought into the world had ever held hands in the womb, twinning, like these two of yours had been doing and are even trying to do now.'

Joyce had just finished being busy with the twins on the baby trolley when they all jumped with surprise as the fire alarm suddenly sounded and all the lights dimmed, but didn't go out.

'Well bless my soul,' Pat exclaimed, 'another first. No, I don't mean the fire alarm, it's the twins. Look! Look at them! They're glowing! They're actually glowing with a sort of luminous light.'

And sure enough, both twins were visibly glowing in the dim light of the delivery room.

'Your two children are obviously very special babies,' she said. 'You look after them and their mother carefully Mister Knight. I can feel it in my heart, there's something very special about these two, your twins…Yes, I sense they really are somehow magically special, very special twins.'

Nurse Joyce, smiling and nodding, agreed, as she carefully passed both babies to Bill.

At that moment the door opened and a white-coated man with a stethoscope hanging round his neck took one step into the room. 'We've got to evacuate this section of the hospital now, sister,' he instructed. 'The incinerator has overheated for some reason and as it's situated in the basement directly below this block, it could prove to be very dangerous.'

'Thank you, doctor,' Pat replied. 'Come on, Joyce, we'll go and find a wheelchair for Sylvia. Bill can bring the twins on the trolley.' And with that, both nurses scurried off up the corridor to the right.

'Somebody is shouting you, doctor,' Bill said.

'I didn't hear anything,' replied the doctor.

'But I did!' Bill insisted, as he had seen a faint dull red glow in the doctor's eyes when he came through the door into the dimly lit room. 'Please have a look,' Bill said, 'it might be a life or death situation.'

With that, the doctor grudgingly said, 'All right, to keep you calm, Mister Knight, I will go and have a look. I'll then come back for the twins to take them to safety. The sister and the nurse will be back to look after your wife and yourself.' And with that, he went to the corner a little way up the corridor.

As the doctor left the room, Bill moved the trolley away from the door to the other side of the room. He then quickly and nimbly vaulted over the bed and grabbed the pillowcase containing the quietly struggling goblins which he gladly handed to the doctor when he re-appeared in the doorway.

'Sister Pat said the twins would be all right in here for a little while,' Bill lied. 'Here they are doctor,' and handed him the pillowcase containing its two wriggling occupants and saying, 'look after them, won't you.'

'Oh yes!' grinned the doctor..... **'I'll look after them all right!'**

He turned and left in a hurry, tightly clutching the pillowcase and went round the corner to the left. Ahead of him he could see where the hatch down to the incinerator was situated in the wall of the corridor. Between himself and the hatch the water sprinkler was doing its best to put out the non-existent fire. Pausing for a moment, he put the pillowcase on the floor to enable him to pull his white coat over his head in an attempt to keep dry.

At that moment the fire alarm stopped ringing and the water sprinkler stopped working. The doctor, now no longer needing his head covered, pulled his coat back off his head, straightened it and picked up the pillowcase. He then called towards the incinerator hatch. **'I've got them. I've got them both here. You can have them now!'** And gave a hideous laugh. But unfortunately for him, what he hadn't noticed was that some of the goblins' green snot had seeped out of a corner of the pillowcase when he put it down, and it now formed a little puddle on the wet floor of the corridor.

The doctor's weird laugh was short-lived, for as he stepped forward he unsuspectingly stepped on to the leaked pool of snot on the wet floor. His surprised yell ended abruptly when, having lost his balance as his feet shot from under him, and having slithered down and forward, he hit the wall beneath the incinerator hatch with a resounding and painful thump! Fear then sprang up in his face and his eyes flickered from red to yellow and back to red again as two huge muscular smoking red arms with scaly and clawed hands, terrified him as they emerged through the hatch. Feeling around blindly, one hand grabbed the pillowcase while the other roughly snatched up the doctor. 'No! No! Not me!' he shrieked in sheer terror. But both arms and hands then returned the way they had arrived, disappearing back into and down through the hatch. The doctor received a huge whack on the head as he was helplessly dragged through the hole, his legs wildly kicking.

His terrified screams continued for a few seconds then abruptly stopped. The brief silence which followed was then crudely broken by a deep belch and a disgusting fart.

Bill, who had been peering round the corner in the corridor and who had watched it all happen, smiled and turned to go down the corridor to rejoin his family. On his way back, he amused himself by saying out loud, 'I'm pleased about what just happened. Whatever it was down that hatch, it got triplets for its supper, not twins, and certainly not our special twins.'

Back in the delivery room, and in an effort to protect the twins, Bill had put them into their black carry-all bag.

'Aw! Don't they look lovely?' Pat remarked. 'And don't they look cozy in their dad's bag, and they are still holding hands!..... It's just magical,...really magical!..... Put the bag on the trolley, Bill and I'll push them. You can bring your wife in the wheelchair and we'll see if we can organize a nice cup of tea and a couple of biscuits for her when we get her in the rest ward. I think if anyone deserves one tonight, she most certainly does!'

Bill nodded and smiled. He was now a much happier and thankful husband, and also a very happy father as he pushed his wife's wheelchair down the corridor. In fact, they were a very happy mum and dad, following Sister Pat pushing the trolley bearing their very special twins. A sister and brother who Sylvia and Bill had already decided would be called Mary and David.

Thankfully their twins had arrived safely. Now, with the help of the Gods of the Terrestrial Light, they would significantly in fifteen years' time, become the Terrestrial Twins. But more about that later as the story unfolds and the magical adventures really begin for all the Knight family, but particularly the twins.

Perhaps the magpie poem could now be changed a little.....to finish.... *Three for our girl, four for our boy.*

Chapter Three

THE ADVENTURES BEGIN

Almost fifteen years had passed since the twins had been born, and the four Knight family members were all in a good mood as they were en route for a two-week June holiday near Moatcaster in Castershire. They were also going to celebrate the twins' fifteenth birthday on the Summer Solstice.

'What's this big secret and surprise all about that's going to be part of our holiday then, Dad?' David asked. 'It's been briefly mentioned a few times, but Mary and I still don't know what it is.'

'Yes,' Mary said, 'what's so important, and why such a mystery, Mum? You said you would tell us when we got to Castershire. But why not now?'

'It's no good you two keeping asking,' Sylvia replied. 'Your dad and I have said on a number of occasions we would tell you all about it when we got to the holiday cottage, and we will. But not until then.'

'So leave it there,' Bill said, joining in the conversation.

'But, Dad...,' David started to speak again.

'That's enough, David. No more! We'll be at the cottage this afternoon and we'll tell you all about it then. We're going to break our journey and have lunch near Forest Valley. We'll then spend a little time in the Forest before going on to Castershire. So, until we get to the cottage, please.... no more!'

'Okay! Dad,' David replied rather cheekily, 'I can take a hint. It seems like that's the way it's got to be!' And he sat back in his seat and started to fiddle with his tablet.

Mary, who had also picked up hers during her dad's little chat, was also sitting quietly using it. The twins knew about the fortnight's holiday in a cottage, but the secret they had wanted their parents to tell them about needed to remain a secret for a little while longer. It was too big and too important to gloss over quickly. Their parents knew it would also take a little time for the twins to be able to absorb and accept what they were going to be told. Traveling in a car at the start of their two week holiday was hardly the right time or place.

Their holiday was planned to coincide with Mary and David's fifteenth birthdays on the Summer Solstice. And it promised to be a day which would be like no other. Neither of the twins had any idea they were to shortly learn that on their birthday they would, and in an amazing supernatural midnight ceremony, become the Terrestrial Twins; but more about that later.

David was a perfect example of the phrase, 'Like father, like son'; likewise, his sister Mary, 'Like mother, like daughter.' The physical training and the many skills they had been taught and practised over the years to help prepare them for what was probably going to be, at times, quite an ordeal, had also helped them both to physically develop into young images of their parents. David was a well built and handsome teenager and like his father had raven black hair. Mary being David's twin sister was also a teenager and attractive like her mother. Her hair, like her mum's, was ash blond, almost white.

Bill was enjoying driving their recently acquired new car, a black seven-seater, which like its predecessor was displaying their Seven Magpies Martial Arts Studio logo on the two front doors. All four of the Knight family looked particularly smart too, wearing black polo shirts and caps, all of which were displaying the seven magpies motif, including the bum bags the twins and their mum were wearing. They were also all wearing matching black tracksuit bottoms and black and white trainers. They were not only a close loving family, but also a formidable team wearing their favourite strip!

The four of them were trained, experienced and fully qualified martial arts experts. To Bill, a Grandmaster 9th Dan, and Sylvia, a Master 5th Dan, it was their business as well as being fun. To David and Mary, who also took it very seriously as they both were black belts 2nd Dan, it was also great fun, as had been the swimming, fencing, riding and climbing, off-road driving and the motorcycling lessons they had enjoyed ever since they could remember.

Neither of the twins realized that their childhood activities had not only been hobbies and fun for them, but had also been part of a strategic plan. An important plan put together by their parents to help to prepare them for just about anything that the Black Arts or entities from the Other World might throw at them. They were not yet aware that the physical skills they had learned and the standards they had reached would help them survive. They had no idea that they were shortly to become the central characters in such an important mythological prophecy.

Bill easily found a place in the car park to park their car when it was time for lunch, and they trooped into the little café to get some.

'Let's not sit too close to a window,' Mum said. 'It might get too hot in the sun.' But that wasn't the real reason. She was just being a protective mum, knowing that out there, somewhere, were evil entities which would do anything to kill the twins if they could.

'Will this do here?' David asked, sitting at a table that was set with four chairs.

'That's novel,' Bill joked, 'a chair each,' then sitting down opposite David, went on to say, 'Your mum and Mary are popping to the loo first, so we'll have a look at the menu.' As there were two on the table they each picked up one.

'They've got sausage, mash and peas, Dad. I love bangers and mash. Can I have that please?' David asked.

'OK, Son, of course you can,' his dad replied, 'and I think I'll have the same. What about a drink?'

'Orange will be fine for me thanks,' David replied.

'Right,' Bill said, 'and I'll have a coffee.'

They both stood up as Sylvia and Mary returned to the table, and it was obvious that Mary was quite excited about something.

'Have a look at that old lady in the corner,' she said. 'I think she could be a witch,' and she put her hand on her mouth to cover up her giggling.

'Don't be rude, Mary,' her mum said, 'she can't help her appearance. You want to thank your lucky stars I don't look like that, or hope you don't when you're her age.'

'It wouldn't bother her at all if she did, Mum,' David joked, as he had also rudely stared at the old lady. 'She'd just jump on her broom and fly off looking for a black cat and a toad.' Giggling to himself, he then walked off with his dad. He too was excited when they returned. 'I think Mary was right, Mum, she could be a witch. She looks just like the ones you see in books and films.'

At that moment the old lady surprised them when she suddenly appeared at the side of their table with what looked like salt and pepper pots made from gnarled old wood, and in a squeaky high pitched voice said, 'I noticed there was no salt or pepper on your table, I have finished eating now so you can have mine.' She then walked out of the café and disappeared.

Sylvia, having said thank you, then as she was doubtful about using either of the two pots went on to say. 'As salt's not good for you kids, we'll not bother to use them,' and turned and put them on the table behind.

They all decided to have and enjoyed bangers and mash and David ate all of Mary's peas as well as his own. He then apologized in advance after having eaten so many, hoping that it wouldn't cause a problem in the car later. They left after having another look at the old lady who was now standing a little way from the door of the café.

Bill allowed the twins to jump into the car first and holding Sylvia's hand said, 'You've got to agree with the kids, love. She really does look like a witch. Possibly she was there as a spy listening to our conversation.'

'If she is or was,' replied Sylvia, '**they** are going to know we are now going into Forest Valley for you and David to do a spot of summer fishing while Mary and I have the bike ride we have both been looking forward to enjoying.'

'We'll just have to be on our guard then,' Bill said. 'We daren't tell the kids anything yet, that's got to be after we get to Castershire. So let's just be careful....'

Later that afternoon, Bill turned off the road on to a track in the forest which he knew from previous visits led to a place where he would be able to park reasonably close to the edge of a fishing lake. He knew that he and David would then be able to enjoy one of their family's favourite relaxing pass-times: fishing.

'I've been thinking, Dad,' David mused as they arrived near the lake. 'Perhaps they're filming a re-make of *The*

Wizard of Oz or something here in the forest and that old lady was an actress having a lunch break.'

Bill laughingly replied, 'I don't think so, Son, not really. But let's forget about her and get the fishing tackle out and enjoy the afternoon. We can also get the girls' bikes out while we're at it, we can then all enjoy what is such a lovely day.'

But Bill thought again about the old lady's appearance and what Sylvia had said earlier and remarked, 'You want to thank your lucky stars we look normal, David, and don't look like that old lady.'

'**Normal!**' David said loudly and laughed. 'We're hardly normal, Dad. Mary and I are twins, but her hair is virtually white like Mum's. My hair is black as a raven like yours. Don't you think we're a bit different to most people?'

Bill laughed and said, 'All right, Son, I take your point. But yes, I really know just how different and special you both are.'

'Don't go soft on me, Dad.....'

Sylvia interrupted. 'Okay, you boys, thanks for getting the bikes out. Now go and enjoy your fishing.'

'And don't fall in,' Mary jokingly shouted to David, as she and her mum hopped on to their new pink folding bikes.

'And don't you two get lost either,' David shouted back.

'We're a good family, aren't we, Dad?' David said, as they reached the side of the lake.

'No, Son. We're a lot more than that, we're a great family! We all care about and love each other,' his dad replied. 'Let's hope it will always be that way.'

David looked a little puzzled, but just shrugged his shoulders and said as he turned towards his dad, 'I'm going to try my new pike lure today. I've put that new braided line you got for me on my reel, but I'm a bit puzzled as to why twenty five pounds breaking strain?'

'Well,' Bill replied, 'you have to expect some branches in the water when fishing under trees, so as we are here in the forest you need to have a stronger line than normal, in case you get caught on any snags. You're less likely to lose your new lure with the stronger braid line.'

'Thanks, Dad, I never thought of that,' David said as he stepped on to a wooden staging from which he had chosen to fish. His dad set up his chair and gear about twenty feet to the left of David.

'It's a great day for the race isn't it, Son?' Bill remarked, as he stretched out and crossed his legs.

'What race, Dad?'

'The human race, Son,' Bill jokingly replied. David just smiled and cast out his line.

A minute or two later David excitedly shouted, 'Fish on, Dad!' delighted he had hooked into something on only his second cast using his new lure. But as he moved to the front of the staging there was a horrifying and shocking splintering sound as the right hand corner of the planks collapsed, pitching him head first into the lake.

As David went in, two huge red-eyed rats slipped quietly into the water from under the staging and grabbed hold of his fishing line in their mouths. David felt such a fool as he went in, an idea flashing through his mind as he guessed his mum would be unhappy with him for getting wet and dirty. His dad had a little laugh to himself, saying out loud, 'David, David!' and shaking his head slowly in an amused manner.

But David was now anything but amused. He could see and feel what was happening but was powerless to stop it as the rats had so quickly wrapped his strong line round his body, pinning his arms tight to his side. Within seconds his legs were also being tethered together. He now had a real problem. The smile quickly vanished from Bill's face too when he realized his son was in trouble. David was a great swimmer, so why had he not surfaced?

As Bill dived in, four magpies that had been perched near where father and son had chosen to fish also dived into the lake. Remarkably, as they hit the water, they magically transformed into four otters.

Bill swiftly covered the short distance under water and seeing his son's predicament, he grabbed and lifted him high enough for his head to be clear of the water to allow him to get some air into his lungs.

Holding his son close and treading water to keep them both afloat, Bill watched in amazement as the rats were chased off by the otters. He was even more amazed when the otters returned and in seconds had bitten through enough pieces of the evilly wrapped fishing line to enable David to clamber out of the lake with his dad.

The otters having left the lake shook themselves and transformed back into four magpies and flew up to return to their perches. His face wet and streaked with mud, Bill looked up at them and said, 'Thank you, *Four for our boy*!'

Meanwhile, Mary and her mum, having ridden off down the track on their bikes, had to stop suddenly when a tree alarmingly fell across their path. A little spring which was bubbling water across the path where they were now standing had formed a puddle, a bit bigger than a hearth mat, and both of them were now involuntarily standing in it. 'What.....what made it do that, Mum? What do you think made the tree fall?' Mary asked in a nervous and shocked voice.

But Sylvia didn't get a chance to answer, for making a horrific squelching, rumbling and groaning sound, the section of wet path on which they were both standing suddenly collapsed. They both then alarmingly and helplessly fell into a hole the width of the path and almost eight feet deep. Their bikes, from which they had so terrifyingly been pitched, were now perched precisely across and over the edge of the hole above them.

In the hole Sylvia quickly found herself up to her chest in a torrent of gushing dirty water that appeared to surge along an underground river. Gripping Mary's right arm tightly with her left hand, Sylvia fought as hard as she could to keep their heads above water. But the force of the water dragging against Mary seemed to have other ideas and she was in danger of being sucked under and drowned.

Sylvia desperately tried to grasp on to the side of the hole with her right hand in a vain attempt to clamber out, but it was all too muddy and slippery. Her clawing attempts, breaking some fingernails in the process, were futile. All she could do was to yell for Mary to hang on to her as she did her best to wedge her legs across from one side of the hole to the other in an attempt to support the pair of them against the incessant current of the water. She then instinctively and loudly shouted, 'Help! Help!'

Moments later she became aware of movement above them and could barely believe her eyes. Three magpies were hovering over their heads, holding on to and lowering her bike down for her to grab, which she gratefully did. The magpies then, with totally unbelievable ease, magically moved up like helicopters. They lifted the bike with the two very dirty and wet female members of the Knight family gripping tightly to each other out of the hole. Sylvia and Mary were then carefully lowered on to the dry grass a few yards from it. The magpies, having squawked three times, then flew up to perch on the branch of a nearby tree. At the same time both the hole and the fallen tree vanished as quickly as they had appeared, with what sounded like a disappointed grunt and a moan.

Then together, as though they had rehearsed it, Sylvia and Mary both looked up at the magpies and said, 'Thank you! Thank you very much!'

Sylvia then turned to her daughter, and trying to make light of the situation said, 'You look disgusting!'

'You should see yourself, Mum,' Mary jokingly but nervously replied, as they got on their now grubby new bikes to go back to the two male family members.

Sylvia looked back at the magpies, smiled and thought to herself, *Three for our girl!*

As Mary was completely at a loss as to what had just taken place, they rode back the short distance they had come in silence. As they walked round the rhododendron bush near where Bill and David had been fishing they came to a standstill. The four of them looked at each other in turn, and could hardly believe their eyes. What a sorry, wet and dirty sight they all were.

Putting his arms round his wife and pulling David and Mary to them, Bill said quietly and calmly, 'Okay, it seems we all have been involved in and experienced some very strange and evil events here this afternoon. But this is obviously not the time or the place to have a long conversation about them as we don't know who or what might be lurking about. We need to get out of here, and get out now! So I ask you two to please be patient and we'll discuss it all later when your mum and I can and will explain everything. I promise! But until then, please, please help us all by remaining patient for just a little while longer.' The twins were understandably still in shock as they looked blankly at their parents. But nodding, they agreed.

Sylvia followed on saying, 'Yes, let's all stay calm and quickly load up. Doing so will help ensure we get out of this forest as soon as we can. Your dad can put the heater on in the car for a while to help us all dry out, and we'll head for the main road. We'll then drive non-stop until we get to our holiday cottage.' Then, and trying hard to humorously defuse the obvious tension, she finished off by saying, 'I'm glad we all left our caps in the car, or we would have probably lost the lot!' With that, they quickly and quietly re-loaded their car and left the area; behind them the seven very helpful magpies seemingly waved goodbye from their perches.

Because the twins were tired, having not slept very well the night before, plus the added shock and efforts from their horrific and virtually epic escapes amongst the trees, they both fell asleep before they reached the end of the valley. What they both then missed was an unbelievably outstanding and amazing supernatural awesome event.......

Having driven a little over halfway through the Forest Valley Road Tunnel, their car was suddenly lifted completely off the road where it then became totally engulfed in a brilliant glowing ball of white and pale blue shimmering light. It then quivered and silently disappeared......

Chapter Four

THE MYTHOLOGICAL STORY EXPLAINED

In what was only a micro-second later, Bill and Sylvia blinked their eyes with both surprise and pleasure when they realized they had materialized outside their Castershire holiday cottage. Not only that, they were both dry and as clean as a new pin, including their Seven Magpies casual outfits they had been wearing when they were involved in the frightening events back in Forest Valley.

They decided to leave the twins sleeping in the car while they unloaded some foodstuffs and boxes into the cottage. Sylvia then prepared coffee for everyone. Bill, having returned to the car for more items and to wake the twins, gently shook their shoulders. At the same time he noticed movement occurring in a couple of bushes in the garden.

David and Mary were also as totally amazed as their parents had been to discover how clean they were, and hear about the supernatural event which they had missed in the tunnel. They could only look at each other in bewilderment and disbelief.

'Come on you two,' Bill said in a warm voice, in an attempt to get the twins to re-focus their mystified minds, 'your mum's making us coffee. We're all going to sit quietly for a minute or two, then your mum and I will tell you everything. You will then be able to understand why those scary events in Forest Valley occurred.'

'Everything, Dad? You're going to tell us everything?'
Mary said her voice full of excitement.

'Yes,' Bill replied, as they all seated themselves
comfortably on the rose patterned three-piece suite. It was
fronted by a wooden coffee table on to which Sylvia had
placed four mugs of steaming coffee and a plate of mixed
biscuits.

'Not before time though, Dad, is it?' voiced David,
and finished with, 'not the coffee and biscuits. I meant the
everything.'

'You've both been very good about it really, very good,'
their mum said, 'especially as we have all been involved in
things today that defy any normal or rational explanation.
However, you will have to bear with us while your dad
and I tell you why these things are happening to you, and
some of what is yet to happen.'

'**You mean there's going to be more?**' David questioned
in a raised shocked voice.

'Yes, there will be,' replied his dad, 'but from now on,
especially after you have heard what we have to say, all
four of us will be more ready for them.'

'Who or what the hell are **them**?' Mary asked nervously,
as she subconsciously reached for David's hand.

'Please try to be calm,' Sylvia said, 'we can then get
started. Your dad and I realize it's all quite bewildering
for you both, but you will fully understand once we've
finished explaining.'

'We're both sorry we raised our voices,' David said
apologetically, 'but come off it, Mum,' he paused.
'Hell......**them**!'

With that he leaned forward to pick up his mug for
a drink. As he did, he touched the attractive deer antler
handled knife lying on the table next to his mug. His highly
tuned reflexes then instinctively kicked in, and he threw

himself back on the settee as the knife, which had taken them all by surprise, had incredibly lifted itself from the table and flown straight at David's head. Fortunately, his martial arts training saved him as he quickly bobbed to the left to avoid being stabbed in the eye.

After hovering for a second or two, the knife, having decided to change targets, shot straight at Mary. She, as David had, also skillfully avoided it. The knife having missed its target for the second time, briefly quivered in the air before having another go at David. This time he not only avoided it, but also hit it with a glancing blow. As a result of the contact, the flying knife bumped on the back of the settee which deflected it towards the old Welsh dresser, where it embedded itself in the wood.

Their dad, seizing the opportunity, athletically vaulted over the settee and grabbed the knife. '**Take the top off that milk, love,**' he shouted running into the kitchen. His wife was close behind him with the twins following on her heels. Bill jammed the pointed knife blade hard into the wooden kitchen table, and then of all the things he might have done, he simply and surprisingly pouring some milk over it. The twins were totally amazed by his actions! But they didn't have long to wait to see why he had done it. For as soon as the milk ran down the length of the knife, there was an immediate reaction. The knife shuddered, and gave off a high pitched hurt whine as it melted down like a bar of chocolate would do if placed on a very hot surface. It then reduced to nothing more than what looked rather like a small pool of green snot-like goo.

'That's got the little so and so,' Bill said, as their mum wiped it off the table with some kitchen roll.

'One thing that surprisingly kills them, believe it or not, but of course you saw what it did, is milk. I don't know why, but milk is fatal to them.' The twins just stood and stared. Again they were totally amazed. Even gob-smacked!

Then they all returned quietly to the comfort of the three-piece suite, David and Mary now even more ready for further explanations.

'**Them**,' Bill said, 'or should I say **they**, are King Offalmire's goblins, evil entities which sadly have the ability to change themselves into almost anything. Their job is to protect their leader, the King of the Other World, by destroying anything or particularly anybody who is seen as a danger to him. Anyone or anything they see as a threat.' On hearing this, an awesome expression of disbelief spread across the twins' faces.

'But then why, why did it try to kill **us**, me and Mary?' David asked in a nervous and apprehensive voice.

Bill looked at Sylvia first, then back to the twins. 'Because as yet unknown to you, and as part of a mythological and supernatural plan created centuries ago, you David and you Mary, are not just our twins. You are destined to become the Terrestrial Twins.

'You, and only the pair of you, in about thirty hours time on your fifteenth birthday, and in a magical midnight ceremony, will inherit and be blessed with superhuman powers and abilities by the Gods of the Terrestrial Light. They are the protectors of all terrestrial, earthly beings, namely human beings. Having been blessed, you will then become the only humans with sufficient capabilities to hopefully be able to defeat King Offalmire, the King of the Other World, Master of the Black Arts. In doing so, you will prevent him from stealing the important Thirteen Treasures of Britain.'

The expression on the twins' faces was now a sight to behold. But they remained silent.

Bill continued, 'The Thirteen Treasures are supernatural items which were hidden by Merlin centuries ago in an invisible secret crystal tower, and he is the only person who knows its location. He concealed them until, or if, they might ever again be needed by mankind.

'Those magical items, if misused, could give King Offalmire the evil power and ability to possibly destroy all that is good in life in Britain or even on Earth as we know it. You two are the central part of this mythological plan and the only two people, as I have said, special twins, who will hopefully be able to stop him. That is why you David and you Mary,' he paused… 'you two are the threat! ….That is the reason your mum and I are both sorry to tell you, is the reason he is trying, if he can… to kill the pair of you, also possibly me and your mum.'

The expression which had developed on the twin's faces was now beyond description, and their now wide open mouths might have caught flies.

Mary tried to say something. 'But….. but…..' she trailed off, not really knowing what to say, but instinctively again reaching for and gripping David's hand, which resulted in both of them experiencing a tingling glow that even showed on their faces, and they immediately and surprisingly felt a lot better.

'That's a weird feeling,' David said.

'It was more than weird, I thought it was great,' Mary agreed, a beaming smile spreading over what seconds before had been a very sad and tensely worried face.

'And I feel a lot better for that too,' David said. He like his sister now was looking more relaxed and feeling a whole lot happier.

'That was the start of your twinning experiences,' Bill said, 'you are destined to have and take advantage of lots more of those.'

David then continued where he had left off. 'It's all so awesome, Dad!..... It's still all so very hard to believe and to accept. But after that little episode with the knife and what you have just told us, and that twinning stuff, I promise you I am all ears now.'

'You might not have been if that knife had lobbed one of your ears off,' Mary jokingly said with a little laugh.

It was obvious they both were now feeling a lot better and ready for more information. Bill was about to resume talking when he noticed two magpies settle on the fence just outside the window and thought to himself, *Two for joy*.

'You will always be supported by both your mum and I, but also by the magical magpies you met in Forest Valley. They have now, for want of a better word, become your guardians. But you two as the Terrestrial Twins will be the ones that matter. You are the only ones who will be given the supernatural powers to enable you to become capable of fighting and hopefully defeating the different evil beings, and possibly some criminals you will meet.

'**Fight evil beings! What kind of evil beings? What sort of things will I be expected to fight, Dad?**' Mary blurted out in a very upset and loud stressed voice.

David then joined in totally unexpectedly. He too was now rather wound up. '**God, Dad! It's all getting a bit too much for us to accept. In fact I can't, I really can't accept it! To me it's all beginning to sound,.....sound like a load of.....and I'm sorry.....a load of fizzing unbelievable rubbish!**'

Bill, raising his voice stopped him. '**David! Enough! That's enough!** There's no call for language like that. Now apologize to your mother and sister!'

David sat back, his chin on his chest looking both glum and confused. Then turning to his mum and sister quietly said, 'I'm sorry, Mum, Mary. But it's all getting a bit weird.' He paused, 'No, a lot weird, and it's also scary, especially when you consider everything that's happened today. It really is getting to Mary and me. I can sense what she's feeling.'

'I'm sorry too, Son,' Bill said, 'I had no idea we were going to have problems today, and I realize that's not helped. I knew having to tell you both and the pair of you having to absorb and accept everything wouldn't be easy, but you just have to listen. You have **got** to accept it! If you two, and I'm sorry to have to say it, if you two are to survive the next few days, you really have to listen.' The twins looked sick.

'Again, as I have said, you both will inherit and be blessed with supernatural abilities at a midnight ceremony on the Summer Solstice. Also when you become fifteen, you become the Terrestrial Twins. Those unbelievable abilities will then enable the pair of you, whether you like it or not, to hopefully complete the tasks I have spoken about. Those tasks that you are mythologically destined to face.'

Bill paused, and reaching over to hold David's right hand and Mary's left hand, he then continued. 'We are powerless to change anything, it really is your destiny. You are the central part of a mythological event as big as anything that has ever occurred or possibly will ever happen.'

'But how do you know all this?' started David.

'Yes,' interrupted Mary, 'how can you, ordinary people, our mother and father, know about.....well, about goblins and.....'

Bill stopped her, saying, 'We have just told you it has all been mythologically planned for you for a very long time.'

'Yes, Dad I heard you, but how do **you** know?' she again asked.

'I was about to come to that, love, but you keep interrupting.'

Mary, saying she was sorry, slumped back.

Bill continued. 'The information we have has been passed on and down through the family generations. You and David will now inherit the knowledge which was passed to us by our parents, grandparents, great grandparents and so on from when they were white witches. Some would say wizards. In fact, would you believe, Merlin is in your mother's Family Tree.'

The twins once more looked astounded.

'White witches are the opposite of black witches who delve into black magic from the Other Side and the evil Black Arts. They, shall we say are the baddies. White witches are good witches, but your mum and I are no longer involved with a coven so no longer practise the arts of white witches. But having said that, it was no accident that you David were born with black hair like mine, and Mary was born with virtually white hair like your mum's. Because of who you are, you will both have even more strength when you become the Terrestrial Twins. When black and white are linked through the powers of the Terrestrial Light and you call upon the magical supernatural power source of twinning, that's linking hands and or minds before asking for help, you will have it granted. You will also gradually develop other almost unbelievable supernatural and remarkable abilities that you are going to be blessed with, and a few you'll find that are truly mind-blowing.

'Your mum's hair being white and mine being black, and you two being born on the Summer Solstice are not just coincidences either. As our families were before us, we four are all part of this centuries old mythological, supernatural and very important plan. Even some of nature's animals that have black and white colours, such as magpies, badgers, dogs, seagulls and even cows, can magically be part of the future in this, your special supernatural destiny.

Apart from both of you being able to call upon and use what are your own special black and white supernatural linked powers, you will also be able to tap into those of the seven friendly and very magical magpies. They will always be around somewhere keeping an eye on you. Now you will be able to understand the significance of the seven magpies in our lives and why we named our business after them.'

The twins looked at each other for what seemed like ages before David spoke. 'But it still is literally an awful lot for us to have to take in though, Dad, isn't it? And what about this Offalmire guy? Is he really as wicked and evil as you say he is? And are you sure when we have become the Terrestrial Twins we might be able to beat him?'

'Yes, I am confident that together you two will be able to defeat him,' Bill replied, 'but only time will tell. You will find after becoming the Terrestrial Twins that by twinning, you will be able tap into the knowledge, wisdom and magical supernatural abilities your mum and I have told you about. Also, your mother and I will never be far away, and you know we are both more than capable of helping. I am also confident there will be others out there just waiting to assist us with their knowledge and abilities.

'As for how evil King Offalmire is, he really is a monster. A total sadist! For hundreds of years he has delighted in hurting both animals and people, but usually in a parallel time zone, and has been known to roast or boil them.'

With that, Mary, closely followed by her mum, rushed to the bathroom with her hands over her mouth......

The twins had now been made aware of their destiny, but what was going to happen next? Would there be any more attempts on their lives was the thought that passed through all their minds as they prepared to go to bed. Might King Offalmire's goblins or some other entities try something else before David and Mary became the Terrestrial Twins; and what about after the ceremony?

From what the twins had been told, it sounded as if their magical adventure had now really started......What next...?

Chapter Five

'BRILLFANMAGICAL' AND 'MAGNORMOUS'

Bill and Sylvia were both pleasantly surprised and pleased that there had been no sign of goblins during the night, but just to make sure they had taken it in turns to sleep. Mary got up just after her mum and dad and, having emerged from the bathroom, David went in and closed the door as Mary went into the kitchen.

It was then that Mary saw **them,** and could hardly believe her eyes. They were two small apparitions that looked something like greyish-blue rats with heads shaped like toadstools and split spiky ears. They had no tails and strangely their bodies were completely hairless. Bill had described their faces to Sylvia, after he had seen them in the hospital when the twins were born, as looking as though they had run into a wall or the back of a bus. Mary spotted them as they were about to put something into the jug of milk her mum had prepared for breakfast and which she had left on top of the fridge in the kitchen, so she yelled, **'Mum! Dad!'**

At this outburst, the now scared goblins made a squeaking noise and jumped down behind the fridge. Sylvia, who had just taken a vacuum cleaner out of the broom cupboard, having spilt some sugar, came running in, the cleaner still in her hand. Bill burst in through the back door, having been outside the cottage checking the car, and joined his wife. '**WHAT IS IT?**' they both shouted at the same time.

'What's happened?' Bill asked as his eyes quickly searched round the room.

'Two horrible little creatures were about to put something into that jug of milk,' Mary said, pointing to the top of the fridge. 'They jumped down the back of it when I shouted, and I think they're still there.'

'Where's David?' Mum asked.

'He's in the bathroom,' Mary replied.

'Okay, then he's all right, so let's see if we can get them out before they can do any of us any harm.' And with that, Sylvia plugged in the vacuum cleaner and switched it on. 'Here love,' she said, passing the tubes of the cleaner to Bill having pulled the brush-end off. 'Let's see if you can get the little, can I say beggars, up and out.'

Bill, squeezing his face close to the wall to get a better view, lowered the tubes down behind the fridge and was delighted to see the little wriggling goblins sucked in. They shot up the tubes, whizzed through the hose and plopped into the cleaner's dust bag. They were now pretty upset, noisy and sneezing. 'I think they might be swearing at us,' Bill said.

'I think I might if I'd been sucked up like that, 'Sylvia jokingly remarked.

Bill then opened the cleaner and removed the bag with its wriggling, sneezing and squealing contents and headed for the bathroom.

David, who was just stepping out of the shower as his dad came in, quickly grabbed a towel as his mum and sister followed.

'Dad! Mum! **Mary!**' he retorted, as they followed each other in. 'Can't a guy have some privacy..... Oh, and I'm sorry, Mum, I've left the seat up and I haven't flushed the loo yet.'

Their Dad then really surprised the twins by saying. 'All the better. You might not believe it, but anything that is or was part of you or your sister is lethal to these little, er, blighters,' and he emptied the wriggling, squealing contents of the cleaner bag into the toilet and flushed it.

What then sounded like choking more than squealing emerged from the loo. Then there was only the sound of the toilet system refilling.

'And no comment from anybody,' Bill said.

'I'll go and clean up that sugar now,' Sylvia remarked.

'I'll get back to checking the car,' Bill said.

Jokingly Mary remarked, 'I'm not in a hurry to go anywhere at the moment.'

'**Out!** Get out, and let me get my dressing gown on,' David insisted. Mary then left the bathroom but didn't close the door. 'Sisters!' David remarked as he closed the door. 'Who'd 'ave 'em?'

A plan of events and places they were to visit that day was discussed over breakfast. 'The problem we have now though,' Bill said, 'is that we really can't safely plan or say anything without **them** knowing where we intend to go and why. We know they are shape-changers, so we have no idea what they might look like from one minute to the next.'

'Let's just go sightseeing then,' Sylvia suggested. 'We can show the twins some of the interesting places we have enjoyed in the past, and possibly have lunch in Fishington.'

Bill, thinking it was an excellent idea, agreed.

They packed a picnic tea into the car along with a couple of blankets to sit on, then tossed in their jackets and caps just in case there was a change in the weather.

'Where are we going first then?' asked Mary, a little excitement in her voice.

Bill replied, 'There are a number of great beaches and castles in the area, and we will no doubt see many of them, but your mum and I are both particularly fond of Moatcaster Castle.'

'Why, Dad? What's so special about that one?' asked Mary.

But before they could answer, David interrupted saying, 'I bet that's where you used to go courting, isn't it?'

Their parents looked at each other and smiled.

'We couldn't afford to keep paying the entrance fee to do that,' Bill said, 'but it is a very important place to us, and yes, romantic.'

'It's where your dad proposed to me,' Sylvia said with a big smile on her face.

'But why in Moatcaster Castle, Dad?' David asked.

'It's simple really if you think about it, Son,' Bill replied. 'My surname is Knight, which meant when we married, your mum would become a Knight. So I thought it would be both a good and romantic idea, as well as the right thing to do, if her own special and favourite Knight so to speak, me, proposed marriage to her in her favourite castle.'

'I think that's lovely,' Mary said.

'And there will be four Knights entering the castle when we go in today,' David said proudly. 'It already feels good.'

Bill was lucky as he managed to find a place to park near the castle. 'Wow!' David said as they approached it.

'And double wow!' Mary said. 'It's huge!' 'Brillfanmagical is the word that springs to mind,' David surprisingly remarked as they entered on the drawbridge over the moat. 'There's no wonder you like the place. It really is..... Brillfanmagical!'

'Is that a new word, love?' his mum asked, a big grin on her face, as they walked on to the grassed area inside the castle after leaving the pay box.

'Yes, it is,' smiled David. 'It just came to me, Brillfanmagical. This place really is, Mum.'

'David's right though, Mum, it really is a wow place,' Mary said, a big smile having spread all over her face too.

Sylvia, still smiling, turned towards David and asked, 'What's that word again son?'

'Brillfanmagical,' David replied as he kept walking ahead towards the huge tower, repeating the word in his mind. He just kept staring at and walking towards what was in fact the impressive Keep of the castle, an almost 60 feet high impressive circular stone, oak-roofed building known as the King's Tower. 'Brillfanfagical,' David said again out loud as the family members joined him. 'What an impressive building it is, Dad. It really is.'

'I'll not argue with that, Son,' Bill replied.

'But there is something about it that feels really odd to me,' David said, 'something.....something special. Something very special! I don't know what it is or why, but it simply somehow feels..... magical.'

'I know what you mean, bruv,' Mary said, 'I can feel it too. What was it you called it?'

David again repeated the new word, but this time with an air of mystery in his voice. 'Brillfanmagical.'

'There are all sorts of places to explore here, even some dungeons,' Bill said, 'in fact the castle is a really interesting place. It has a maze of mysterious tunnels, corridors, staircases and passages in the walls and a variety of different kinds of rooms.'

But David was in no mood to go anywhere else at the moment. 'I have to look inside here, here inside the King's Tower,' he said to himself.

As though reading his mind, Mary added, 'Me too.' And in they went together.

David took Mary by the hand as they walked through the door and they again both experienced that warm friendly yet unusual sensation they had experienced the day before. 'I like this twinning,' David said.

'Me too,' Mary replied. 'Fancy us doing it when we were in Mum's womb. That was really cool.' As they were now wearing their caps, they had to turn them round back-to-front to be able to look up at the carved oak timbers which covered the Keep's roof high above them, which almost gave them a crick in the neck.

Suddenly, although her surprise appearance didn't frighten either of the twins, a misty hooded figure, an old lady in fact, appeared out of thin air just above their heads then slowly descended in a beam of pale blue light. Having stopped to hover about a foot from the stone slab floor, she then pointed at each sibling in turn and speaking quietly said, 'You both had problems in water as you journeyed to Castershire. I now remind you both to always be aware of water, also water witches and witches in the sand!' She then faded, and was gone.

Bill and Sylvia appeared in the doorway only seconds after the old lady had vanished. Unaware of the visitation, they were greeted by a big grin on David's face. 'This is the spot where you proposed to Mum, wasn't it, Dad?'

With surprise in her voice his mum replied, 'How on earth did you know that?'

'I just felt it,' David said looking around. Then he continued in a serious voice. 'This is where I am going to propose in about four or five years' time, or even less.'

'I think we had better get these two out of here quickly,' Bill said jokingly. 'It must be the Castershire air that has affected him.' And out into the courtyard they all went.

'The King's Banqueting Hall, or so it is called, is over this way,' Bill said, 'and your mum and I know you would like to see that.'

The twins' mum then continued with, 'It's a huge room on the first floor of this partially ruined building. It's built into and forms part of the wall of the castle, and it's said to be the home of a mythical dragon.'

'Legend has it that a supernatural invisible dragon moved in when the castle fell into disrepair. It moved in after the family who owned it moved out more than two hundred years ago, and it's been in the Banqueting Hall ever since. We can climb up the spiral staircase in the adjoining Queen's Tower and have a look in it if you like.'

'Yes please,' the twins eagerly said together, 'that would be ace!'

They were about halfway up the narrow stone steps, Bill bringing up the rear just in case anyone slipped, when David and Mary came crashing down into him. Fortunately, he hadn't been taken by surprise and was able to catch hold of them both, preventing either of them from possibly going any further down and having a nasty fall.

'I was tripped over and pushed at the same time,' Mary blurted out.

'And I was tripped too as she bumped into me,' David gasped.

'They're here then,' Bill said in an angry voice. 'Do you want to continue up?'

'We're not letting **them** spoil our day out,' David replied in a forceful and manly voice.

'No, we're not,' agreed Mary just as decisively.

'Okay, then let's keep going up. But let's be very careful.'

The twins couldn't believe their eyes when they emerged from the stairs and through the arched stone doorway into the room.

'It's…..it's huge,' Mary said in an amazed voice.

'Brillfanmagical!' was David's not unexpected reply. 'It really is Sis…..in fact…… it's……it's magnormous!'

'That's two new words from you today, Son,' Bill said. 'What was the second one again?' Bill asked grinning.

'Magnormous,' David replied. 'It really is both brillfanmagical and magnormous.'

The King's Banqueting Hall really was enormous, and except for a long oak table about 10 feet from the huge fireplace and a grill covered latrine chute in an alcove, it was totally empty. Its warped creaky wooden floor was about 150 feet long, by something like 75 feet wide and the room was quite dark. A single set of lights suspended from the timbered roof about 40 feet above them and shafts of sunlight piercing through the four small windows along the Queen's Tower side of the room were the only means of illumination.

David spoke first, 'I can imagine a dragon being really happy living in this big room. If I was an invisible supernatural dragon, I would love to live in here. I could use that table as a pillow. It would be great.'

A few comments were passed about the huge fireplace, and not surprisingly about the latrine chute and the cleverly woven wall tapestries, before they decided to leave. It was just before they had reached the top of the staircase they were all surprised to hear a noise from behind them, a sound rather similar to that of a horse snorting or coughing.

'What was that?' Mary enquired in a surprised voice.

'It's that invisible dragon,' David said jokingly. 'It sounds like he's got a bit of a cold.'

Bill joined in the joke. 'Well, it is a bit cool and damp in here. I think I might catch a cold if this was where I lived.'

They looked at a few other places in the castle including the dungeons, then left.

'Where are we going to now, Dad?' David asked.

'Were going to visit the beautiful beach at Serpent Dunes Sands,' Bill replied. 'But we'll stop at a couple of places en route, as there are a few things we would like to show you that you might find are a bit special too. Let's hope we can have an afternoon without problems.......'

Chapter Six

THREATENED BY OFFALMIRE'S GOBLINS

Having driven along winding narrow roads that gradually took them uphill through some rather attractive green and sometimes bushy and tree-spotted countryside, the Knight family arrived on the outskirts of a small village.

'We're going to stop here for a minute or two,' Bill announced as he stopped the car opposite a little grey stone church. 'This is the highest ridge in the area and you can see for miles.'

The panoramic views were wonderful and they all enjoyed a peaceful few minutes looking around and chatting about the attractive scenery and what they could see.

'The RAF camp I was stationed at is that way, down there.' Bill pointed towards RAF Keepfield.

'This is St Field's,' Sylvia said as she turned to face the church, and with a smile on her face continued, 'this is where your father and I were married.'

'Really, Mum?' Mary remarked, a beaming smile having appeared on her face as she now looked more intently at the stone building. The church possibly could best be described as no more than an average looking country church. It had a tall, square castellated tower at the west end and an old porch entrance that had seen better days. But Mary's up-bringing showed when she politely said, 'It's a really lovely church, Mum. Can we go in?'

'Yes, love, we can if it's unlocked. Your dad and I had planned before we left home that we were going to go in anyway. So yes, we all can go in together.'

Once inside, the twins' parents slowly strolled to the front of the church, leaving David and Mary admiring the stained glass window in the south wall. As the twins felt their parents would like a private moment, they moved out of the main part of the church and into the old porch. They had barely stepped out of the church when out of nowhere they were frighteningly confronted by a shabbily dressed, wizened old hag pointing an evil looking three-pronged pitchfork at them. Trying to take evasive action, the twins were horrified to discover their shoes had somehow become glued to the floor and their bodies were completely paralyzed. Neither of them could move a muscle. It had all happened in the blink of an eye, and they now were completely at the mercy of the scruffy old woman who was obviously preparing to kill them.

The hag was just about to plunge the fork into Mary, who was unfortunately standing closest to her, when the twins were yet again amazed. A black and white border collie dog suddenly appeared behind the old hag. In the blink of an eye it amazingly grew to four times its original size before lunging forward and roughly grabbing hold of the old hag by the head. Having violently shaken her and unceremoniously smacked her down hard three times on the stone floor of the church porch, it ran off with the now lifeless hag hanging from the side of its mouth. It then disappeared just as quickly as it had arrived, and at the same time Mary and David's feet and bodies fortunately returned to normal.

'It's a lovely church isn't it?' Sylvia said as she and Bill rejoined the twins who were now slowly walking back to their car, desperately trying to shake the image from their minds of what had just occurred, and also sensing that neither of them wanted to tell their parents.

'Yes, Mum,' Mary replied, 'it is a lovely church.' Having managed to raise a smile, she continued, 'We can understand why you and Dad liked the idea of calling in for a little visit.'

Their mum then surprised them by reciting a short poem she had learned from her grandmother. 'When you have time and see a church pop in and pay a visit, so when you enter God's pearly gates he won't need to ask *Who is it?*'

Mary replied, 'That's lovely, Mum, I'll try to remember it,' and looking at David continued, 'even if my brother doesn't.'

David then embarrassed her a little when he repeated the words perfectly and grinned.

'We're now going down to show you the entrance to RAF Keepfield,' Bill said as they drove from the church. 'As I have told you, it's the RAF camp where I was a physical training and unarmed combat instructor. It was while I was stationed there that I met and got to know your lovely mother and where she also became a martial arts expert.'

'Yes, I was working in a little shop on the camp at the time,' Sylvia said.

'Look at those two jets,' David excitedly said when they slowly drove past the front of the camp where there was a Hawker Hunter aeroplane parked on either side of the entrance.

'It was a great camp,' Bill said, 'especially as I met your mum there. But those jets are a bit special as well. They represent the fact that the Hunters in one form or another have been active in the Royal Air Force for more than fifty years. The camp's been here much longer and the main part of the airfield is built on a peninsula, a strip of land that juts out for almost a mile into the sea.'

Bill continued talking as they drove the two miles towards the village of Keepfield, the village from which the camp had taken its name. 'There are loads of caves in the cliffs which form the peninsular on which the runway was built. Your mum and I visited and explored most of them, especially those the sea penetrates, as we were able swim and dive into them. But there are obviously quite a few which have never been explored by civilians for security reasons, as they form part of the boundary of the camp.

'I bet that was great fun, Dad,' David and Mary together found themselves saying, and laughingly pushed each other.

'We are now about to enter Keepfield village,' Sylvia said. 'This is the village I lodged in when I worked on the camp.'

'Do the people you stayed with still live here?' Mary asked.

'No, love, I'm afraid they don't. Sadly they both perished in a mysterious fire the night I had to work late in the shop to do some stocktaking. No one ever came up with an acceptable explanation as to why there was such a fierce blaze. It was as though Bob and Wendy, that's who I stayed with, had both spontaneously self-combusted. The fire chief said it was good fortune that I wasn't there at the time, as I normally would have been, or it might also have happened to me. But our families didn't think it was an accident. Everyone thought that I had been the real target, but sadly for Bob and Wendy, I wasn't there at the time.' There was a brief silence while everyone felt a little sad.

'Your dad and I are just going for a short memory lane walk down there,' Sylvia went on to say, pointing to a road on their right as Bill parked the car at the side of the road.

'It's only a small village, kids,' Bill said, 'so I'm afraid there's nowhere for you to go. You can either wait in the car, as we'll only be a few minutes, or perhaps you might go back and explore that square stone walled area behind the monument and phone box we have just passed. The small area inside the wall used to be a pen, locally called the 'Pen Pound'. Many years ago, animals that had strayed were kept in it to be collected by their owners. At the start of World War Two they fitted machine guns in it to protect the road to the camp, but all there is in it now is a mock-up of an old gun set in a rather pleasant garden. You could go and have a look in there while you mum and I have our short walk. It will give you something to do for a few minutes. We won't be long.'

The twins decided the pen might be worth a visit. The moment they entered the stone walled garden the twins experienced an uncanny and eerie feeling, and both nervously jumped when they were startled by two jackdaws flying up from the border in which they had been feeding.

'It's creepy in here,' Mary said in a quiet, nervous voice.

'You can say that again,' David replied, 'but I don't understand why? It's only a small stone walled garden with three benches and a mock-up of an old gun. But you're right, Sis, it does have a strange and eerie feel about it. Those two jackdaws flying up and those rooks flying overhead and calling out don't help either though, do they?'

But there was no doubt about the eeriness of the place, and for some inexplicable reason they both were experiencing feelings of apprehension. It did feel a very spooky place.

Then, and literally out of nowhere, they were suddenly and frighteningly surrounded by six ugly rat-like pug-nosed knee-high creatures, similar to the ones they had flushed down the toilet. They had simply materialized out of thin air and, for what seemed like ages but was only a few seconds really, they stood staring at the twins with beady, glowing, evil red eyes. Then slowly and menacingly they began to circle around them. The twins were once more under attack and again frozen to the spot. Two of the goblins then even more frighteningly started to grow in size until they were as tall as David. Then together they picked up a very large stone that at one time could have been the capping stone of an old fireplace. The twins were both amazed and fascinated to see the arms of the two goblins holding the stone unbelievably begin growing longer and longer, enabling them to lift the stone up and right over the twins' heads.

'What can we do?' asked Mary, her voice understandably nervously trembling as neither of them could move and they once more were being threatened.

'This,' David replied! And grabbing hold of both of his sister's hands he yelled, '**PLEASE! CAN YOU HELP US?**'

The goblins were so surprised by this outburst, they stopped circling and the two holding the big stone wobbled. At the same time, they were all surprised and amazed to see the wispy figure of a silver haired and smiling old lady in a white cotton, ankle length gown simply drift out of the wall, in what can best be described as a bubble of pale blue shimmering light. Addressing the goblins she said, 'Now! Now! Now! This won't do at all! This peaceful garden is a place for people, humans, not evil goblins. You have absolutely no right to be in here. I suggest you go now, immediately, and leave these twins alone. Believe me, the consequences of your not doing so will be,' she paused, and smiled, 'shall I say...... be grave.'

The long-armed goblins holding the big stone just grunted, totally ignoring her remarks and lifted the stone even higher as though to drop it on the twins.

A sort of shimmering bright light then shot out from the forefinger of the right hand of the lady's now outstretched arm and enveloped the large stone and both long-armed goblins. Then, whoosh! They were both hurtled across the garden to land with a sickening crashing bump against the wall. The huge stone abruptly silencing their screams as it fell with a dull thud, squashing them to a pulp. The twins watched in amazement as what looked like a puddle of green snot slowly oozed out from under the stone.

With another circling movement of her hand, the old lady then treated the four remaining goblins to a similar fate, but without crushing them. They simply squirmed, squealed and slithered as they too became no more than little bubbling puddles of slimy green mucus.

'Don't worry about that stuff,' the old lady said pleasantly and calmly. 'The insects and the magic in here will soon get rid of all that.' Smiling, she continued, 'That's a lot better now though, isn't it?' I do hope you both have an enjoyable birthday and are totally successful in your endeavours over the next few days. You should then be able to enjoy a good holiday with your mum and dad. But you must watch out for water witches and witches in the sand.' Then she faded through the wall and was gone. Again, they had received another similar warning.

All the twins could do was look at each other in silence with blank expressions on their faces, having yet again had such a magical and unexplainable experience.

'And what did you think about the garden?' Bill asked when their parents returned from their walk.

The twins looked at each other before Mary spoke for them both. 'It was all right I guess. But we weren't keen on that circling stuff.' And they both had a big smile on their faces.

Bill then drove out of the village and happily headed towards Serpent Dunes Sands.

'The road drops down ahead as we drive over the hill, so keep looking forward and you'll get your first view of your mum's and my favourite beach. We call it the surprise view.' And a surprise it most certainly and sadly was!

They had just started descending the hill towards the sharp bend high above the beach on the top of the cliffs when Bill loudly exclaimed, 'NO! NO!'

'What's wrong, love?' Sylvia asked in a stressed voice.

'It's the brakes! It's the ruddy brakes, love! They're not responding and it's a steep hill and a sharp bend. I need them! And the damned handbrake isn't working either!'

Not only were the brakes not working but the car was also being supernaturally accelerated and the steering was locked. Bill couldn't do a thing, not even turn off the engine!

Their car was now speeding faster and faster down the hill towards the cliff edge, and there was absolutely nothing he could do about it...They were terrifyingly totally out of control! The twins and their mum couldn't help screaming out loud when they also realized the car would not be able to safely continue round the sharp bend they were approaching, high above the rocky beach. All they could see ahead of them was blue sky, azure blue sea and jagged rocks almost 300 feet below!

With a final terrifying, neck-jerking bump on the edge of the verge, and a yell from everybody, their car, having hit the side of the road at such speed, was catapulted up and out as though it had been shot from a cannon. Totally out of control, it plunged horrifyingly over the edge of the cliff.......

Chapter Seven

PRIMROSE ISLAND

Apart from the sound of the racing engine there was an awesome silence for about three seconds in the Knight's car after it shot over the edge of the cliff.

Then, somehow, everything thankfully changed. Their car's awesome forward and downward plunge amazingly and suddenly stopped, throwing all the family forward and testing their seat belts. They then realized that their car, having stopped falling, was now being held and suspended in mid air.

David, in a high pitched still frightened voice, was first to speak. 'It's the magpies!' he shouted. 'Those wonderful magical magpies. Not seven, but dozens of them.....Look!'

And sure enough, unbelievably, their car had what is known as a huge parliament of magpies holding on to it by every bit of whatever they could get at to grip.

Their car was fortunately fitted with substantial roof rack strips and it was on to these, as well as the mirrors, the four wheels, wheel arches, grills, and anything else they could hold with their feet, that the magpies were gripping. Their supernatural strength had given them the ability to magically catch and hold the car. Now, having literally caught it in thin air, they gently lowered it into a car parking space in the viewing area cut into the hillside overlooking the sea.

After carefully lowering the car and squawking twice, *Two for joy*, the magpies simply vanished.

Looking at each other, the Knight family all seemed to agree there was no point in trying to talk through the unbelievably terrifying incident. So they said nothing and accepted it as another awesome, supernatural and extremely frightening event from which they had again been helped to escape and saved. There was no doubt, the Gods of the Terrestrial Light were definitely with them and protecting them!

They sat quietly for a few minutes, each with their own thoughts. Again it was David who broke the silence. 'I bet nobody else has seen Serpent Dunes Sands from that angle before, Dad.'

'Not and lived to talk about it,' his dad replied, and continued, 'I had said earlier that this beach is one of mine and your mum's favourite places and you'll soon see why. There is a bigger car park halfway down the beach road, opposite the sands, and a café which has an ice cream and hot dogs bar. There are also public toilets to the rear of the car park and some amusements on the far side. So let's drive down and have a look at it. I think the car's all right now. The engine and brakes are functioning as they should, so we'll drive on and park in the main car park.'

'An ice cream would be great,' Mary said, 'but I think the toilet is a better idea first.' Everyone nodded in agreement.

'Oh, Dad…… you were so right,' Mary said as the sands and dunes came into view, 'it really is a beautiful beach. Just look at all that gorgeous golden sand and the sand dunes at the far end. It's wonderful! It all looks really inviting.'

'Is that somebody surfing?' David asked.

'Yes,' Bill replied, 'surfers regularly use this beach, and there are also about two miles of this gorgeous sand and the sand dunes for anyone to enjoy. The naturally occurring waves make it a very popular beach for surfers so they regularly come to ride and compete on them. However, there can be a bit of a downturn in the area, as it isn't called Serpent Dunes Sands for nothing. We need to be aware that we may come across an adder when we're in the sand dunes, as there are a lot of them in this region. They aren't really a problem though, they are just something else we need to watch out for, as well as possibly unwelcome entities.

'One other thing you also need to be aware of is, as the sand is so very soft, it can be a bit of a problem when it's covered by water. It's a bit like quicksand in some places, so let's all be very careful.'

'I think it would be a good idea if we all changed into shorts,' Sylvia said. Everyone agreed and they changed in the toilet building, returning their tracksuit bottoms to the car before buying an ice cream to take with them to the beach.

Bill then led the way down steps opposite the end of the car park and pointed to a small island about the size of a block of four houses, which looked as though it had been plonked on to the sands about 150 yards from the base of the cliff. The tide was going out and had almost cleared the far end of the island, which pleased both Bill and Sylvia, as it meant they would be able to show the twins how to get up and on to it.It was a place where they had enjoyed many hours lying in the sun together, and was known by locals as Primrose Island.

'We used to have some fun here,' Sylvia said, as they reached the right side of the island. 'Your dad and I used to paddle and try to catch fish in this very pool. We regularly came for walks down here in the summer or on warm evenings and at weekends.'

'Look!' David said. 'It's still got some fish in it. We ought to have brought a little net,' he said as he floated a piece of driftwood out on to the pool, imagining it to be a small boat.

'It's this way to get up,' Bill said, leading the way. 'The whole area is volcanic rock, and as you can see, in some places on this side of the island it virtually forms natural steps. If you ever come up here on another occasion, remember you have to keep an eye on the tide. Or you might find you have been marooned. Me and your mum once were and had to wade back in water up to our waists.'

For some reason Sylvia found the story a bit embarrassing and asked Bill to 'leave it there', so he changed the subject and talked about the natural steps. They all carefully followed him up until one by one they stepped on to the short grass that grew on the flat top of the little island.

Looking around, Mary said, 'What a beautiful picturesque view. It's quite breathtaking, Mum. There's no wonder you and Dad liked it so much.'

'We loved it here, Mary,' she said, putting her arm round her daughter's shoulders. 'We still do and always will.'

'Looks like somebody has been trying to make a fire up here, Dad,' David said, kicking at a little pile of broken and partially burnt driftwood. He then tripped, his foot getting caught in an old rabbit hole as he leaped back with a yell. **'A SNAKE! Dad, there's an adder!'** he shouted, as it quickly wriggled towards where his bare leg was defenseless on the grass, his foot still jammed in the rabbit hole.

Bill grabbed a shoe-sized rock as he flung himself to his son's rescue. The snake was only inches away from David's outstretched leg when its head was split open by the rock in his dad's hand.

'Thanks, Dad,' David gasped. 'But that's a heck of a snake.'

'That's no ordinary adder, Son,' Bill replied as it liquified and turned into a pool of green mucus. 'I think we had better get back down while we can, just in case there are any more hiding up here. We can't afford to be too careful. King Offalmire's entities seem to be everywhere.'

Both his sister and mum had witnessed what happened and agreed a hasty retreat would make a lot of sense. They all had one last look round at the attractive view, Bill taking a few photographs, then carefully descended and returned to the beach.

Back on the sand they spread their blankets in front of a large rock which conveniently supported their backs.

'I will be glad when tonight is over and you two have gone through the full twinning process and become the Terrestrial Twins,' Bill said. 'So please, please let's just try and see the rest of today over without any more,' he paused...... 'life-threatening incidents!' Everyone agreed.

'But we can't promise anything,' David laughingly called back as he and his sister walked off towards the edge of the sea to explore the pools amongst the rocks and enjoy a paddle. What could possibly go wrong?

Chapter Eight

THE OLD LADY'S WARNING

As the twins went off to explore, Sylvia and Bill laid down on the blankets Sylvia had brought with them to help make them more comfortable on the beach. Opposite where they were laid, the rocks protruded at an angle from the sand and ran in parallel lines all the way from the head of the beach out to where they finally disappeared into the sea which was lapping and breaking over them. As the strips of sand between the rows of rocks was in places covered by pools of water left behind by the tide, and the rocks were raised on either side, they looked a bit like naturally formed dykes.

Pools of seawater as we all know are what most children and the young at heart would consider to be ideal paddling pools. The twins were no exception, so it wasn't long before they had removed their trainers and were enjoying paddling in and exploring the pools.

Mary had gone a little way ahead of David when she cried out to him. 'DAVID!' There was a ring of panic in her voice. He wheeled round not knowing what to expect, and was shocked to see his sister almost up to her waist in wet sand.

'DAD! MUM!' he yelled. 'Mary is stuck in the sand!'

Looking at the situation as he got up, Bill picked up one of the blankets, and with Sylvia hard on his heels they raced to where their twins were.

'I've tried but can't get to her,' David said, 'this area has turned into quicksand.'

'Try not to move, love,' Bill said addressing Mary. 'Wriggling could make you sink further down.' But by now she was almost up to her chest. 'Right, David, jump onto my back.'

'What the hell for?' David said in a shocked voice.

'Just do it, Son, and you'll soon see why.' So David obeyed. As soon as he was on, Bill handed him the blanket saying. 'Whatever you do, don't drop it!' Then facing his wife he tightly clasped both of her hands, and they twinned. 'If you shuffle on the rock along that side, love, and I move along the rocks on this side, we will be able to form a bridge over Mary. David can hold on to one end of the blanket and lower the other end for Mary to grab hold. We should then be able to pull her up and drag her out.'

They then carefully edged and shuffled their way along the protruding rocks until they did in fact, partially thanks to their fitness and strength, form a human bridge above Mary. 'Right,' Bill said, 'now, David, lower the end of the blanket to your sister but **don't let go of it!**'

David had just started to lower the blanket, when up out of the sand from a crevice in the rock emerged an ugly little creature, best described as a female goblin. She was even able to walk on the water towards Mary, who wisely made no attempt to try to hit her in case her movements made her sink deeper. The goblin then grabbed the end of the blanket with one scrawny hand, while at the same time trying to push Mary's head under the water with the other. Then, in a cackling voice said, 'There is no escape from water witches and the witches of the sand.' Both twins then remembered the earlier warnings.

But David was now in danger of losing his grip on the blanket as it was continually being pulled and tugged by the evil, ugly little witch.

Suddenly and seemingly out of nowhere, a huge black and white seagull waddled up behind the witch. She had no idea she was in danger until it was too late. The gull picked her up, smacked her three times against the rocks and laid her down on some seaweed. It then proceeded to cover the evil little witch with another piece of weed before picking her up between the layered pieces. It then threw its head back and, in one go, gulped down the lot.

Mary, now being free of the little witch was able to reach up and grab hold of the blanket. David then slipped down his father's back onto the rocks to lighten the load, at the same time passing the end of the blanket to his dad. His mum and dad were then together able to slowly pull Mary up and out of the wet sand and to safety.

They all waved and called 'thank you' as the very friendly, very helpful seagull squawked twice, *Two for joy*. Then flying out to sea, it disappeared.

Sitting down on the blanket when they returned to where they had left the other one, Bill, wiping the sweat from his forehead said, 'What next, kids? I honestly thought the event on the island was to be the last, but it looks as though **they** still don't intend to let either of you live until midnight for the twinning ceremony. You're lucky to still be alive. You might not be so lucky next time, if and whenever that might be. So please, please be careful!'

'We'll be all right, Dad,' David said confidently. 'I've got Sis, and we've got you two, and I'm sure either the magpies or something else magical are around somewhere keeping an eye on us. What more protection could we have or need?'

'The important question now is,' Mary said, 'where are we going next?'

'A **more** important question,' David said, butting in, 'is where do we go for the ceremony?'

Bill answered them both at the same time, 'I was going to tell you later when we were on our way, but seeing as you've asked I'll tell you now. The midnight ceremony will take place at an ancient megalithic site called Fulsi Chamber Stones. It stands on a hill a few miles inland from a lovely coastal town called Fishington, which has a gorgeous harbour. As I mentioned earlier, we will be calling there today for lunch before we visit the stones.'

'What was it that you called the place, Dad, a megalithic something?' David asked in a puzzled tone. 'What on earth is one of those things?'

But Mary butted in. 'I know. It's one of the things that cropped up when I was surfing the net before the holiday. I wanted to find out something about Castershire before we came and that's when I found it. It's an ancient burial place really. It's a site and structure that the druids and others seem to have sort of adopted over the years because of the mystical things that have been recorded as happening there, or near there. Some have occurred close to it and in its circle of stones, others happened amongst its raised stones.'

'It looks like your sister's got one up on you there, David,' Sylvia remarked, a big grin showing on both hers and Mary's faces. David just shrugged his shoulders saying, 'Okay, so we're off to Fishington first and then that other place. That's fine with me.' And with a broad grin on his face he continued with, 'Even if it all sounds a bit fishy.'

Having been smiling all the way as they walked back to the car, David's sense of humour got the better of him and he began to giggle, which then turned into a chuckling laugh.

'What's so funny?' his mum asked.

'I was just thinking about that big helpful seagull,' David replied.

'And?' Mary enquired.

They all then joined in with David's laughter when he said, 'I think it really enjoyed eating that particular **sandwitch**.'

Chapter Nine

THE AFTERNOON BEFORE THE SUMMER SOLSTICE

The route Bill had chosen to Fishington was a pleasant run which took them through some attractive scenery with views of the sea on one side and the Beam Hills on the other. As Fishington is a favourite location for holiday makers, they had a bit of a problem trying to find a place to park when they first arrived, but eventually found a parking spot down a side street just off the main road.

After lunch, and having called in to a few shops to buy necessary tinned and packet foodstuffs and put them in the car, they walked over to have a look at what must be one of the most picturesque old harbours in Castershire. The road descending to the harbour gave them a really good view of it as they walked down, and Bill stopped to take some photographs. Feeling in a bit of a childish and funny mood, David shouted, '**Last one down's a lemon**,' as he raced ahead down the hill past a row of gift shops and a café. Mary close on his heels.

The harbour occupied a natural break in the landscape at the foot of where two hills met. Row after row of white, pink, cream and green painted and stone-fronted fishermen's cottages nestled into the hillside below the trees, overlooking and also along the edge of the harbour creating a tranquil and pleasant scene. The old quay built of slabs of stone was fronted by a handful of boats and a variety of colourful dinghies, their halyards occasionally slapping against their masts as they bobbed about on the small waves lapping against them. With the seagulls calling, darting and weaving it all helped to make a really delightful picture. It was as though a talented artist's painting had come alive. It even looked good to the twins.

'Wow! Look at these old cannons,' Mary said, referring to a semi-circle of five large black cannons standing outside what had at one time been the lifeboat rescue station built into part of the cliff face at the head of the harbour.

'I bet that lot did some damage when they were fired,' David said.

'They certainly could and would have,' Bill added, 'especially if cannon balls and chain were shot out together. Cannons like these were mean pieces of ordnance in their day.'

'Ordnance, Dad?' questioned David.

'Yes,' Bill replied. 'Ordnance is just another word for a cannon or gun.'

'Thanks for that, Dad..... I think,' David mused as they slowly walked away from the cannons and passed a number of small fishing boats as they strolled towards the breakwater at the far end of the quay. Their route took them past a hotel painted bright yellow, a handful of gift shops and an amusement arcade, as they continued along the front of the cottages. They had almost reached the end of the quay when, and without any warning, a huge explosion occurred that echoed all round the bay, literally shaking everything as though it were made of jelly; the sound vibrated in their ears. At the same time, an invisible projectile screamed through the air and ripped through the pile of neatly stacked net covered crab pots they had just walked past, scaring the life out of every member of the Knight family. Some of the pots were even torn out of the centre of the pile and tossed to the other side of the breakwater. About half a dozen were even knocked into the sea by whatever the projectile had been that had terrifyingly ripped through them.

'RUN!' shouted Bill. 'Back to the other side of the cannons. It looks as though **they** have managed to shoot one of the damned things at us.'

They only stopped running when they reached a safe area on the road behind the cannons. 'That was a near miss,' panted Bill. 'They somehow managed to get one of the cannons to fire. We were very lucky that time. I dread to think what might have happened if whatever they had shot had hit us. Let's get back to the car.'

Even though they were super fit, they were all gasping for breath after such a fast run and could only nod in agreement.

Fortunately, the journey to their next location, the ancient megalith, was uneventful.

'We're almost at the site of the Fulsi Chamber Stones,' Bill said, 'we'll have a look at them now, then come back just before midnight for your special twinning ceremony.

'So, to add a little more information to and finish off what Mary told us about the site and of the stones earlier... The Fulsi Stones are thought to be one of the finest megaliths in existence, not only in Castershire, but anywhere. If I remember correctly, the stones are thought to have been positioned around 4000 BC. Most similar structures are thought to have been burial places. Tombs covered in soil. The stones here are now clearly visible, as the soil which originally covered them has either eroded or has been cleared away.'

Sylvia then added, 'And as you said earlier, Mary, such sites have also become places of interest to druids. They hold ceremonies at or close to them, including this one. In fact, they have held rituals around them for centuries. Like so many other similar sites, this particular stone circle and its central structure are steeped in folklore and legend, and all kinds of supernatural happenings have been recorded here. Goblins and fairies have regularly been seen and a so-called 'Blue Lady' has appeared on numerous occasions.'

Bill then added, 'Like so many other similar sites too, large black dogs and cats, and even a lion and a bear, have been reported in the mystical area surrounding the Fulsi Chamber Stones....And would you believe it, here we are.'

'And thank goodness we made it in one piece,' Sylvia added giving a sigh of relief.

David followed on saying, 'Amen to that.'

Bill parked the car in the designated area and, walking slowly, they marvelled at the structure ahead of them as they steadily made their way over to the megalith.

'The stones at this site, like many others, were erected on a hill so that the megalith would be nearer to the sun and moon gods,' Bill said.

They stopped when they reached the nearest stone which formed part of the outer circle of standing stones which was about 60 meters across, and Bill spoke, 'The circle is made up of thirteen almost pear-shaped free-standing stones, each about eight feet tall. Some calendars used by ancient scholars contained thirteen months to make up a year, and it's thought that the thirteen stones in this circle probably have something to do with that, but some other scholars think differently.'

Having looked round the outer circle of stones, they walked closer to the large and impressive central structure of the Fulsi Stones for a closer look. Having reached the huge stones, they all stood quite still, mesmerized by the silent and mysterious splendour of the megalith. They couldn't help mentally absorbing the magnificence of the structure, but not really knowing what to think. The structure and the sensation they felt were equally totally awesome.

The impressive structure consisted of two large vertical stones at one end, and two slimmer standing stones at the other, the four stones together supported an enormous capping stone.

'That capstone across the top,' Bill said, 'believe it or not, has been estimated to weigh between fifteen and twenty tons.'

'It's just brillfanmagical,' David said, 'its magnormous. Can't you feel it? Can't you feel..... feel the atmosphere? It feels.... sort of electric. It's almost like the air is.....sizzling. Yes, for want of a better word, sizzling. It's magically awesome.'

'Yes, I can feel it too,' Mary said, 'it all feels.... it all feels alive. It's making me tingle all over...... Yes, Bruv, it truly is awesome. It really is a magical place.'

'There will probably be some modern druids performing ritual dances round fires at the bottom of the hill when we come back tonight,' Bill said, 'they will be able to *do their thing* outside the megalith area but they're not allowed close to the structure.'

'Yes,' Sylvia added, 'we might see some of them later or maybe some other things.'

Bill continued, 'Both of you will be going through the special twinning ceremony tonight as we reach the hour of midnight and your fifteenth birthdays. The Gods of the Terrestrial Light had arranged it to also coincide with the magical Summer Solstice. It is in that midnight ceremony that you, Mary and David, will become and be blessed as the Terrestrial Twins!

As your mum and I explained to you when we arrived in Castershire, together and individually you will be blessed by the Gods of the Terrestrial Light with special powers and supernatural physical abilities. The unique ritual is a special event which was planned centuries ago. It really is your destiny.'

Interrupting his father, David said, 'Sorry, Dad, but I think we have company,' and he pointed into and under the large stones towards the far end of the megalith. And there, standing towards the rear of the structure between the two narrow vertical stones and looking a little ghostly in a beam of pale blue light stood an apparition of a tall, slim, distinguished looking man. The light by which he was illuminated made his long grey hair and beard look like shimmering silver. He was wearing a full-length pale blue and white smock robe, tied loosely at the waist with what looked like dark brown knotted rope. On his feet he was wearing brown sandals.

Raising his left hand and pointing a finger in the direction of Fishington the man said, 'You must leave now, and return to the place you left this morn. It could be dangerous for you to dwell here any longer at this time. Leave now. Return later at the midnight hour.' He smiled and slowly faded away.

There was silence for what seemed like almost half a minute before Bill said, 'That really got to me! Your mum and I have explained to you how information about the mythological and magical things that are written had been passed down to us through our families. But that was the first and only time your mum and I have actually seen a messenger from the Gods of the Terrestrial Light. I am sure I speak for both of us when I say, apart from being a bit scary, that was something special.'

Sylvia took his hand, 'Yes, love,' she said, 'it most certainly was. In fact, I am sure all of us were moved by that experience. But we must go. We must leave now, right now like the man said, before there are any more problems. I don't want to alarm any of you, but if you look to the other end of the megalith where the visitor was standing, you will see two of those awful damned entities we saw earlier peering at us from behind the supporting rock on the left.'

It only took seconds for the Knight family to quickly retrace their steps to their car, fortunately without any incident and they were soon journeying back to their holiday cottage. They all had a multitude of thoughts running through their minds and mixed feelings of excitement and apprehension, knowing they would later be back at the megalith for the special supernatural twinning ceremony when David and Mary would become the Terrestrial Twins...

Chapter Ten

MIDNIGHT AND TWINNING

It was almost six o'clock when Sylvia, with help from Mary, began to prepare their teas. They had been held up for a little while in a traffic queue on the way back to their holiday cottage due to some road works, just prior to the bridge over Satan's Valley through which the River Glower flowed.

While they were waiting, a couple of shifty looking cyclists wearing slate grey one-piece overalls and huge black boots and dark glasses had stopped on either side of their car, repeatedly glancing in. Normally, this probably wouldn't have bothered them too much, but they were all on edge from the events which had occurred in the last twenty four hours, so consequently had found the experience a little spooky. Fortunately, nothing untoward happened, and they eventually arrived back at their cottage.

'I think we'll all have scrambled eggs on toast,' Sylvia said. And as no one argued, they busied themselves preparing their teas.

Sylvia had just started whipping the eggs in a bowl with a fork, as there was no food mixer in the cottage, when out of the corner of her eye she noticed two goblins. They were creeping on the floor behind Mary who was sorting out the cutlery from the sideboard drawer, totally unaware of their presence.

Both goblins were holding small deer-horn handled knives, similar to the one they tried to slash or kill the twins with the day before. Sylvia, realizing she needed to act quickly to warn her daughter, loudly shouted her name. '**MARY!**'

The goblins had just started hovering close to Mary's knees when she whirled round and to their amazement, and also thanks to her martial arts training, she quickly pressed down with her elbows and forearms on the top of the sideboard and lifted her whole body weight off the floor. This allowed her to safely swing her legs away from the flashing knife blades.Both goblins were then hurled across the room as a result of two well-aimed kicks. And boy, could Mary kick! They only stopped screaming and flying through the air when they hit the wall opposite with two sickening and painful thuds.

Bill, having heard the commotion, had now arrived on the scene. Picking up both very stunned goblins, he tossed them across the kitchen towards his wife who, having smartly caught them, opened the hatch to the food waste disposal unit, and in went the goblins.

David, who had been unpacking the car with his dad, came in. Having seen what was happening, he started grinning like a Cheshire cat, having had the notion to quickly pour a drop of milk into the disposal unit before he switched it on. There was barely a sound from the goblins, only a mixture of choked yells and glugging noises. And that was that!

'You can put the eggshells in as well, David,' his mum said, 'and I can get back to preparing our teas.'

'I'm starving,' David said.

'Me too,' said Mary.

Then Bill spoke, 'We'll have a good look outside, David,

while your mum and Mary finish getting our teas ready. We'll see if we can find any more of the little blighters.'

'I don't particularly want to find any more little blighters thanks, Dad, if you don't mind,' David joked, and they kept checking until tea was ready.

After tea they showered and all looked very smart having changed into fresh sets of their favourite black Seven Magpies strip, including their caps, before setting off for the ceremony.

Bill's driving skills fortunately saved them a couple of times as they journeyed back to the site of the Fulsi Chamber Stones. In both instances a brown clad motorcyclist tried to force their car off the road. On the second occasion, the motorcyclist lost control and shot out of sight into the dark.

'I think that might be the last we see of him,' Bill said confidently, then continued. 'I sincerely hope that was their last attempt. It's very dark now and getting close to midnight.'

Both David and Mary would normally be tucked up in bed and fast asleep at this time, but tonight they showed no signs of being tired even though it had been a very stressful thirty six hours. They were understandably too excited and apprehensive to feel tired. It was nearing the midnight hour and the time for the major event, their very special and supernaturally important Terrestrial Twins ceremony.

It was twenty minutes to twelve on the night of the mystical, and tonight magical, Summer Solstice, and almost the twins' fifteenth birthday when Bill parked their car near to the megalith.

'This is the special event we have been journeying towards since before you two were born,' their mum said, taking hold of Mary's left hand.

'Yes,' Bill continued, as he took hold of David's right hand. And that's all he managed to say, for as David reached out to clasp Mary's right hand with his left, an enormous black bear with red blazing eyes suddenly and menacingly appeared out of thin air in front of them.

Moving remarkably quickly, it charged, attempting to get between them. At the same time it tried to claw or bite them with its long pointed, slashing claws and fang-like teeth. And what an evil dribbling mouthful they were. Fortunately for them, Mary and David's reflexes were faster than the bear's, and it missed. Having turned, and with a mighty blood chilling roar, it raised itself to stand upright on its hind legs. It was massive! A terrifyingly huge, ugly creature. A horrifying hairy mass of malicious muscle. After uttering another bellowing roar, and just after David managed to again take hold of Mary's hand, it began a second charge. This time it attempted to leap at them. Remarkably, having hit up against a thin pale blue transparent barrier which magically had suddenly descended around the four of them, the bear simply bounced off and vanished.

'The powers of the Gods of the Terrestrial Light are now defending us,' Bill said. 'They have banished the dark evil trying to destroy you both and are protecting all of us with their Terrestrial Light, at least for now.'

'But how long is it likely to last?' David nervously asked.

'I have no idea, Son,' replied his dad.

'Me neither,' their mum said, 'but thankfully the bear has gone and it's almost midnight. You two now need to get into position and stand in the centre of the chamber under the capping stone.'

The transparent shield then expanded to engulf the whole of the megalith, and David and Mary, hand in hand, stepped under the huge capping stone into the centre of the structure. This was the very thing that King Offalmire had so desperately been trying to prevent from happening.

Their father then addressed them: 'Now, face each other. Grasp each other's hands in a twinning fashion, then cross your hands over and under each other's.'

Bill and Sylvia, who had now joined Mary and David in the chamber under the capping stone, turned to stand facing each other. They then made the same twinning movements with their hands and arms as they stood facing their twins.

Bill glanced at his watch. It was midnight......

Speaking in hushed voices, Bill and Sylvia together found themselves saying: 'We, as parents of these your chosen twins, call upon you, the Gods of the Terrestrial Light, magically ruling over black and white and all things good, to bless our black and white haired twins now standing in your presence, to enable them become your chosen Terrestrial Twins. Please grant them your special and supernatural strengths, wisdom and abilities through twinning and as individuals to enable them to act in your service, assisting you in your endeavours against all evils for the good of mankind.'

A moment later, a powerful beam of gently shimmering pale blue and white light, accompanied by beautiful soft music, descended from out of the darkness, seemingly cutting through the blackness of the night. As the twins became enveloped by the beam, they too became covered in a similar shimmering blue and white phosphorescent glow. They then experienced a tingling sensation creeping all over and spreading through their bodies, accompanied by a feeling of absolute calm and pleasure.

Looking at each other, they smiled and twice nodding their heads simultaneously said, *'Two for joy.'*

The light and music then slowly faded and the four of them stood quietly and peacefully together holding hands.......

However, mini-seconds later it all horribly changed. There was a terrifyingly awful scraping, creaking and groaning noise as, and without any warning, the four standing stones which supported the capping stone suddenly shot outwards, pushed by some hidden force..... Then, as there was now nothing to support it, with a terrific and horrifyingly sickening crashing thud, the megalith's many tons of capping stone came crashing straight down where the four Knight family members were standing........

Not a sound could be heard as a thin dust cloud spread over the area and settled on the awesomely totally silent ruins of the megalith stones.......

Seconds later, just as he had materialized earlier in the afternoon, the distinguished gentleman with the long silver beard again appeared. Hovering slightly above the huge, capping stone, now lying flat on the ground, he remained motionless in the dark and silence of the night for all most half a minute, his head bowed forward, his chin on his chest.

He then, in a quiet and controlled voice, said, 'Why do the evil ones from the Other World try so hard to spoil all that is good?' And having taken a sprig of mistletoe from inside his robe, he pointed it in turn at each of the four collapsed stones. Then, having slowly drifted to just beyond the two thinner fallen stones, he loudly commanded....'RETURN AS YOU WERE – STONES AGAIN BECOME ERECT!'

As his feet touched the ground, there was a rumbling and crunching sound similar to that when the megalith had collapsed, and all the stones incredibly rose up and returned to the same position in which they had been only minutes earlier. He then disappeared.

As the dust cloud settled, the four members of the Knight family appeared, totally unscathed. They all stood silently looking at each other with bewildered expressions on their faces as they dusted down their clothes.

David said, 'If the new powers given to us by the Gods of the Terrestrial Light having been through our Terrestrial Twinning process can do that for us, I don't think we have too much to worry about. Or do we?'

Moving out from under the huge capping stone, Bill said, 'I think you're right, Son. I should imagine we can honestly now feel a little more confident about the rest of our endeavours, whatever they might be.'

'I wouldn't like to think any of us might ever have to experience something as awful as that again though,' Sylvia said. Mary just looked shocked and nodded in agreement.

'You were right about modern druids doing some traditional dancing, Dad,' Mary remarked, as having returned to their car they sat fitting their seat belts. 'They look like they're all having a good time dancing round a fire at the bottom of the hill.'

'I'm sure they're all enjoying themselves, love,' replied Bill. 'But they wouldn't have seen or heard anything of our ceremony. All we did tonight and the Fishington cannon experience earlier today, or anything else that might happen, did so in our own parallel time slot and didn't or can't affect anyone else. No one could have seen it or have been affected.'

Sylvia broke into the conversation. 'Well, kids, you have now actually become the Terrestrial Twins, but you're still our special twins, and as it's after midnight it's now your fifteenth birthday, so Happy Birthday to you both!'

'Yes,' Bill continued, 'Happy Birthday to the pair of you – and many more of them.'

Having thanked their parents for their birthday wishes, the conversation ended and Bill set off to return to the cottage.

They were all enjoying the view of the lights as they drove across the Satan's Valley Bridge, when, having reached about the halfway mark, and without any warning, they again found themselves under attack......A huge, awesome, towering, whirling and thrashing waterspout frighteningly rose up from the river on the right hand side of the bridge. It smashed up, over and through the fence which edged the bridge and frighteningly whirled its way across the road towards them.

Bill attempted to pull up and stop before it could get them, but sadly he was unable to avoid the swirling, splashing and lashing mass of water as it spiralled at great speed towards them. The towering column of dirty water looked like a black towering, roaring and evil whirling apparition. With a terrifying thrashing sound and bone-shaking force, it slammed into and over their car with such power that it felt as though they had been hit by a truck and began lifting and pushing the vehicle towards the left hand side of the bridge.

They were all conscious that the river was almost 300 feet below them. Now, yet again, there was another real reason for them to feel very frightened. The evil gushing waterspout roaring round them was relentless in its efforts to both raise and push them sideways and sadly, in less than half a minute, it succeeded. The Knight's car, with everyone inside, having been helplessly jerked, pushed, pounded and bounced, was then somehow supernaturally lifted until it finally toppled over the rail of the bridge.

'**Hold tight!**' Bill yelled over the loud voices of everyone else, 'it's taking us over.' Then as quickly as it had arrived, the evil whirling, thrashing water vanished, having successfully toppled their beloved family car off the bridge. And it began the long fall down in the darkness towards the fast flowing river and rocks below......

It was hard to know exactly how far they had fallen before they were rather abruptly brought to a swaying standstill. Except for street lights in the distance and on the bridge above them, it was pitch black, so they had no idea why their plummet had stopped. Yet again, they had been supernaturally caught in thin air, thankfully saved! But how? And by what?

David spoke first in a rather shocked voice. 'What's happened? Why aren't we still falling? What has stopped us?'

'I've no idea, Son,' Bill replied and turned the engine off. 'I just know we have, and I thank the powers that be for doing it, for saving us yet again. But I really don't know how.'

Mary and her mum, still in shock, said nothing. It was then they all suddenly became aware that their car was again moving. The bridge, which they had somehow just been lifted back up to and which they were now above, seemed to be moving away from beneath them. Their car was now definitely travelling forward in the direction they had originally been driving, but now they were gently moving through mid-air about 100 feet from the ground.

A car park in what looked like a large shopping mall came into sight below them, and into this their car was now being very gently lowered.

Within seconds of the car's wheels touching the surface of the car park, and in total surprised shock, the whole family quickly pulled away from the offside of the car, or as far away as their seat belts would let them. Their eight eyes were almost as wide open as their mouths and the whole family had total disbelief written all over their faces......

'My God!' exclaimed Bill. 'It's.....it's a dragon! A huge, red dragon!'

'A real live one!' announced Mary, her face oddly beaming.

The dragon opened its mouth and fortunately, instead of blowing out fire, it amazed them all by speaking in a well-educated voice. 'Would you please be kind enough to lower the windows, or better still get out of your car. I will then be able to speak with you without making too much noise. I would hate to upset anyone passing, as much as they shouldn't be able to, someone just might be able to hear my voice although they would not be able to see me.'

Steadily and nervously unfastening their seat belts, the Knight family members each in turn slowly and gingerly stepped out of the car. Anticipating their concern, the dragon went on to say, 'I am sorry you actually started to fall from the bridge before I caught you! But I had received two emergency call-out messages tonight and yours was my second job. The first one I thought was three large penguins adrift in a boat, but I realized when I rescued them that they were not king penguins at all. They were three nuns who had lost their oars!'

Both David and Mary giggled at what they both thought was an amusing story. 'I usually go for a fly down the River Glower after midnight, especially through Satan's Valley, as doing so allows me to fly low so as not to upset any radar screens, but enough of me. Happy birthday you two! It is my pleasure and an honour to be the first from our world in this region to meet and address you, the Terrestrial Twins. Welcome to Castershire.' The twins glowed with pride and even more so when they grasped each other's hands. 'You came into my place of rest, my home, in the King's Banqueting Hall at Moatcaster Castle. I wanted so much to speak to you then but I stayed invisible so as not to frighten you.'

'Was it you who sneezed?' asked Mary as she found herself walking towards him.

'Yes,' the dragon continued, 'but you will have to excuse me. I would like to have spent more time with you, but perhaps another time. I will keep an eye on you while you drive home and make sure you have no more problems tonight. You all must be tired out.'

'We certainly are,' replied Bill. 'And thank you for so expertly saving all of us!'

'My pleasure entirely, Bill,' the dragon replied. Then, after saying goodnight to everyone and taking a few steps away from Mary, he took off into the dark, leaving the four members of the Knight family waving goodbye and feeling a little bewildered.

'I love him!' Mary said. 'But if we had a big dragon like him, where would he sleep?'

Sylvia amusingly replying, 'I should imagine, anywhere he wanted to, love!'

Chapter Eleven

HAPPY FIFTEENTH BIRTHDAY!

It was almost nine o'clock when the twins emerged for breakfast from a restless night's sleep, and like their mum and dad, were both wearing shorts and T-shirts. Mary emerged first, David following five minutes later. When they were all assembled in the kitchen there was a chorus of Happy Birthdays from their mum and dad.

The twins also exchanged birthday greetings and cards, and thanked their parents for their cards and particularly for the sports watches, something they had both wanted for some time. They then surprised each other when they realized they had both bought the same present, the latest Martial Arts Encyclopedia. But both of them were delighted with their twin gifts and joked about borrowing each other's book.

Then, as their parents had done earlier, they enjoyed eggs, bacon, sausage and beans. Needless to say David found something rude and boy-like to say about the beans.

Drinking the last of his coffee, David remarked, 'Mary and I are the Terrestrial Twins now, Mum. How special is that for a birthday?'

'Yes,' Bill said, 'you most certainly are the Terrestrial Twins, the emissaries of the Gods of the Terrestrial Light and, like them, you two are now protectors of creatures and terrestrial beings of Earth, particularly human beings. Your mother and I are so proud of you and look forward to being able to help you in all your endeavours, whatever they might be.'

'But I don't feel any different though,' David said...... 'do you, Sis?'

Mary laughingly replied, 'No, I don't at the moment, but I've only just finished my breakfast...... But I do have to say how happy I am with my watch and encyclopedia, and I know you are too, David, because you have just telepathically communicated with me and said so! How brill was that?'

A little while later, Sylvia came back into the cottage having pegged out some washing. Then, addressing Bill she said, 'There's something in the bushes out there, love. In fact, I think there are a few somethings in the bushes and in the lane.'

Bill, looked out of the window and laughed as he replied, 'I can see what was in the lane, love, as now it's in the garden. One of the black and white cows from the field opposite seems to have squeezed out or has somehow managed to get into the cottage's garden and is now happily munching on the flowers.'

'Will they upset its stomach or its milk or something?' Sylvia asked with a note of concern in her voice.

'No, I don't think so,' Bill replied. 'Most animals know what's good for them and what's not. I'm sure the cow knows what she can eat. She might just like them.'

He had no sooner finished speaking when the back door burst open to reveal two goblins. Again they were similar to the ones they had previously seen, but these two were much bigger almost as tall as David. But the pair of them were just as revolting as the others had been, with candle-like runs of snot oozing from their noses and heading for their half open mouths.

Bill reacted quickly with a well-aimed flying chest kick as they attempted to enter the kitchen, and expertly floored one. Sylvia, just as expertly, floored the other. But the entities weren't defeated. Surprisingly they quickly leaped up for more. What can best be described as a very active martial arts fight developed and moved out through the back door and out into the garden. At one point it even looked as though the goblins might win, for having put Sylvia down with a nasty kick to her stomach, they both attacked Bill. The twins then joined the fight to help their parents, having first grasped their hands together in a twinning stance.

With their additional strengths, they each attacked a goblin with such veracity and skill that it wasn't long before they had overpowered both their attackers, and firmly pinned them down.

Bill had a brainwave. 'DRAG THEM OVER HERE!' he shouted, towards where the cow had been quietly watching the event. 'UNDER THE COW, DRAG THEIR HEADS UNDER THE COW!' The twins looked puzzled, but did as they were asked.

What happened next was a big surprise to the other three Knight family members, and possibly an even bigger surprise to the cow. For Bill, having taken hold of two of the cow's teats on its udder, seemingly like an expert, then directed squirts of milk on to the faces and shoulders of the pair of groaning goblins.

With their faces horribly contorting, the entities groaning turned to frightened squeals, as the well-aimed milk which had been squirted and splashed all over them took its magical effect. Neither of the writhing goblins managed to escape the teats' lethal milk and, just as the previous entities had, their bodies turned into a thick viscous sludge until after a little while their gooey remains became no more than repulsive, bubbling green mucus-filled muddy puddles.

David was still sitting on the lawn when two more ugly goblins appeared. They were a slightly different and browner colour and more rounded in shape than the first two. One was much taller than the other with particularly long legs; the second one had really short legs. They each then surprisingly managed to grab hold of one of David's ankles. One had his left ankle the other his right, and they began dragging him across the grass. David was at first amused by their antics, but then, and with a look of horror on his face, he realised the entities would be passing either side of the sundial in the centre of the lawn. This meant his legs would also be passing each side of the sundial and the outcome for his crinkly bits and nuts was now looking painfully dangerous.

Fortunately for David, his dad, realizing what was about to happen, rushed to his son's assistance. He jumped on the working end of a rake which was lying on the grass. It shot up, cracking the short-legged goblin which had bent over, in the jaw. The rake then having been deflected sideways, still continued upwards, coming to a shuddering stop between the legs of the long legged goblin, delivering it a blow similar to the one from which David, thanks to his dad, had fortunately just escaped.

Bill and Sylvia then dumped both hobbling goblins, now screaming in pain, into the garden barrow. Grabbing the barrow's handles, Mary then quickly pushed it towards the cow that was still leisurely grazing in the cottage garden.

Whether it was because of the flowers it had been eating, or because of the excitement of the fight, or possibly because it realized it could do it, as Mary reached the rear of the cow, it surprised everyone by lifting its tail and splattered both goblins with evil smelling dung. Fortunately it missed Mary as she cleverly did a cartwheel out of danger.

The dung, having been a product of the cow, had the same effect on both goblins as the milk. Writhing and horribly screaming, they dissolved into a greenish brown obnoxious mess in the barrow.

'You might say they got a pat on the back there!' David laughingly joked. Everyone nodded and smilingly agreed.

As that appeared to be the end of the episode, the mess was cleared up with a brush and shovel, assisted by a garden hose. After showering again, they all changed into their favourite Seven Magpies outfits. 'I'll put the dirty clothes in the washer now,' Sylvia said, as the others put their drinks and bits into the car. 'I can put them out on the line to dry for when we get back. Washing clothes seems to be an almost full-time job. I'm glad they're all non-iron!'

'Where will we be going off to today then, Dad?' Mary asked.

'Believe it or not, we're going to see if we can find Merlin,' was his surprising reply, which brought expressions of astonishment on both the twins' faces. 'We hope we can locate him as we need more details of what is happening, and what his plans might be to get rid of King Offalmire.'

'Find Merlin?' retorted David. 'Can we really do that? Will we really be able to get in touch with him, Dad?'

'Yes, Son, I think we can. In fact we have to, and we need to try and do it now. It is obvious King Offalmire is doing everything he possibly can to get rid of you two.'

'Thanks a lot,' grumbled Mary.

'But will they keep trying, Dad?' questioned David.

Bill replied, 'Yes, Son, I think they will. You two, having become the Terrestrial Twins, are now even more of a threat to Offalmire than you ever were. Remember, he wants to find the Crystal Tower and its hidden Thirteen Treasures. He realizes you two represent the only power, for want of a better word, that might be able to stop him, so you're a threat. A real threat, so he wants to get rid of you. Both of you! So it makes sense we develop a plan to get rid of him before he can get rid of you, if you see what I mean. We rather like our family as it is.'

'But Merlin hid the Thirteen Treasures, didn't he?' replied David. 'So how can Offalmire know where the Crystal Tower is? Or more to the point, how are we going to be able to find it, and how are we going to be able to stop Offalmire if and when he does find it?'

'Yes,' Mary said, 'it's all getting a bit complicated isn't it? There seem to be far more questions than answers!'

Their dad continued. 'Yes, I know it doesn't look easy, Mary, but your mum and I have given a lot of thought over the years as to how we might locate Merlin, and we've developed a plan, well, a sort of plan.' He was then forced to pause for a second or two as he needed to avoid two black clad motorcyclists who tried to cut him off on a bend. 'I'm afraid they're still at it. I've got to keep my wits about me or we might be in trouble.'

He then continued. 'Right, the plan, or should I say the thinking behind it, is this. There isn't only one place, there are in fact quite a number of different locations in Britain where Merlin is supposed to be buried or trapped as a prisoner in magical bonds.'

'Really?' David and Mary spoke together.

'Yes,' Bill replied, 'but we, your mum and I, think the right place is here, here in Castershire.' David's and Mary's faces simply beamed. 'The location is in fact, only a couple of miles north east of Bronzeford, which isn't that far from where we are staying.'

'It's all because your dad applied the logic of one of his favourite phrases. What he calls the "Don't Know" formula,' Sylvia said. 'He has always maintained that if you don't know where something is or what it is, how on earth can you possibly know where or what it isn't. That's why we always so readily turn to him when we mislay things.'

'You clever dad!' Mary exclaimed, and after giving him a big hug went on to say, 'If I remember correctly, what I saw on the web and according to folklore Bronzeford is supposed to be one of the places in which Merlin was born?'

'Yes, love, you are right,' Bill replied, 'but the place we're going to visit is a hill that used to have an old chapel on it. It's known as Badger's Hill. It's the place where, not only your mum and I, but our families who went before us, feel is the place where we may be able to hopefully communicate with Merlin.'

'You've got to be kidding, Dad,' David said in an excited voice.

'No,' Bill continued, 'we think that Merlin, fed up with what was happening around him at the time, purposely tricked the Lady of the Lake into sealing him up. He's not really a prisoner at all. He has simply been waiting for the right event, yours, the coming of the Terrestrial Twins, to help him defeat King Offalmire once and for all. In doing so, he hopes to be able to save the Thirteen Treasures of Britain which he hid inside the Crystal Tower.'

'That's brillfanmagical,' David said, 'you clever people.'

'Let's hope you're right,' Mary said, 'getting in touch with Merlin would make a big difference to everything we want and need to do.'

'We not only think we're right,' their mum said, 'but we have to be. I doubt we'll get another chance!'

Later that morning, having driven a few miles from Bronzeford, they parked their car in a lay-by next to a wooded area on the lower part of a hill.

'Is this Badger's Hill, Dad? ' David asked as they pulled in.

'Yes, Son, it is. What's left of the old chapel is on top. By the look of things, we'll need to go up through the wood to reach the ruins.'

'It's a really nice spot,' Mary said. 'It looks as though it could be a popular picnic area. It's an ideal undisturbed and naturally attractive area in the country and it looks so peaceful.'

'We won't need to worry about people if there are any around anywhere. As I said after your twinning ceremony, most of the things we do occur in a magical parallel time, which means normal people can't ever see or hear what is happening. Perhaps you two can start using your new twinning abilities and see if you can do anything to help us contact Merlin.'

The twins again realised they had yet to use their newly acquired supernatural powers, whatever they might be, so they agreed they would try.

They had gone only a short way into the wood, David and Mary leading the way having again clenched hands and twinned, when out of nowhere roared two scramble motorbikes travelling at high speed and zooming straight at them. The awesome thing about it was that neither bike had a rider. The machines were supernaturally and astonishingly hurtling at them riderless!

A sensible leap to the side was all that was needed to avoid the first attack. The second run however was going to need something different. As the bikes had failed to hit their targets, they skidded and spun round. Still hell bent on causing maximum damage to all the Knight family members, the two entity bikes came roaring back up the hill.

Having quickly weighed up the situation, all four family members were now ready to take evasive action. Mary and David took on the first bike, expertly side-stepping to their right to avoid what would otherwise have been a body smashing impact. At the same time, they both gave the bike an enormous kick. Their mum and dad repeating the twins' actions did the same to the second scramble bike.

Both machines having been slammed into the trees, slowly changed from being bikes into writhing entities, which then melted into pools of green and oil-filled mucus.

'I take back what I said a couple of minutes ago,' Mary said. 'It's not that peaceful here after all.'

'I think that will be the last attempt on us,' Bill said rather optimistically. 'I feel that if your mum and me are right and Merlin is somewhere up this hill, his magic should help prevent any other attack as we get closer to him.'

'I agree with you, Dad,' David said, 'but we had better be prepared just in case we're wrong.'

They emerged from the wood near the top of the hill when the twins, who were again holding hands and leading, suddenly and uncannily, and seemingly for no apparent reason, started to walk away from their parents on the general path towards a collapsed wall and a clump of bushes. They stopped when they reached an outcrop of rock close to a particularly ruined part of what was left of the ancient chapel's west wall, where they were joined by their parents.

David then astonished his mum and dad by saying, 'This is Merlin's home. This is where the portal is to where Merlin has been living. Just as you said, Dad, he's not really imprisoned. He's here, living below the summit of this hill under the ruins of the old chapel. How clever is that! You and mum not only worked it out, you got it right. Spot on in fact. I'm really impressed! Well done!'

'Yes, that was really clever of you both,' agreed Mary.

Then, just like David, she was surprised that she also knew such things and went on to say, 'The portal that David sensed is right here. It's hidden in the entrance to this badger set amongst the ruins and rocks. In fact, a poem comes into mind......' Then seemingly out of nowhere she spoke these words.....

Not Merlin's prison nor place of grave,
Neath rubble of stones sealed in a cave,
He dwells near Bronzeford underground,
By 'Twinning' for Merlin he will be found.

Then, and a little startled by its sudden appearance, they all stepped back a pace. A badger, which slowly increased in size to the height of their mum, emerged from the hole. Having reared up to stand on its hind legs, it spoke to them in a warm and friendly voice.

'Don't be afraid. I am not here to hurt you. You have experienced enough problems with those evil beings from the Other Side. I, like the dragon who helped you last night, would like to welcome you all to Castershire. It is an honour for me to now be able to properly meet all of the Knight family..... You will be my special Knights.

'You and your lovely wife, Sylvia, and your special Terrestrial Twins are now invisible to anyone else. We can talk without being disturbed, but I think you are aware of that fact. Shall we find somewhere to sit?'

While Bill and his family were looking to see where they might sit, they missed the transformation. What only seconds before had been a badger, they now recognised as the same blue and white robed, long-haired and silver-bearded gentleman, the one they had seen at the megalith the evening before.

'How rude of me,' he continued, 'allow me to introduce myself, my name is Merlin.' There was a brief silence as the twins' mouths dropped open in astounded disbelief.

'It is our pleasure and an honour to be in your company, sir,' Bill said, a nervous tremor in his voice. 'We were hoping we might communicate with you somehow, but we didn't expect this, to… to be able to meet with you. Thank you for allowing us to see you and to talk with you.'

'Literally,' David whispered and Mary smiled.

Merlin then went on to say, 'Sylvia and yourself were absolutely right. I haven't really been a prisoner, locked up for many, many years. And as you also cleverly guessed, I did magically trick the Lady of the Lake into thinking she had entombed me in this hill. Where, I must say, I have been very comfortable living with the badgers.

'I decided to transform myself into a badger, as it has been said for many, many centuries, that a tuft of badger hair has the power to warn off witchcraft and demons from the Other Side. So too can black and white or virtually white and black, when blended together. As both you and Sylvia know, Bill, that is why like the twins, yours and Sylvia's hair colours are black and almost white. So I transformed myself into a badger, which is black and white and naturally is covered in badger hair, as it seemed to be a wise move and has helped me many times over the years.

'I have a tuft of badger hair in my pouch for you to keep. You will eventually find it more than useful,' he said as he removed the badger hair from the little leather pouch hanging from his waistband and handed it to Sylvia.

Looking a little taken aback, she said, 'Thank you, Merlin,' and put it in her bum bag. 'I will always treasure it!'

'Now,' addressing the twins he went on to say, 'you two must listen very carefully. It didn't happen last year, but since you became the Terrestrial Twins last night, you, and you alone, are the only ones who might be able to destroy King Offalmire, the supreme evil being. But I am sure your parents have fully explained the circumstances to you. You now have the power to call on anyone or anything you choose, or might want or need to assist you in what will possibly be a difficult and at times a demanding and dangerous task.'

'There is, however, only one thing that can kill Offalmire. A magical poison delivered on the point of an arrow. But not just an ordinary arrow. The arrow and bow **must** be formed from the timber of one of the sacred yew trees found only in the arboretum grounds planted around what are now the ruins of Bowtown Hall. And the arrow must pierce the king's eye.

'The yew trees were planted centuries ago by the region's Bow Master who owned the hall. There are in fact fifty two yew trees, which he planted to form an avenue up to a summer house situated on a small hill on the west side of the hall. Each tree, for supernatural reasons, represents a week of freedom in the year. The avenue of yew trees is the central section of the arboretum, which in turn forms the grounds around the hall.

'The Bow Master, who had been appointed by the king, and whose name escapes me, planted the yews solely for the purpose of making long bows and arrows. As all the yew trees were blessed by the Gods of the Terrestrial Light at the time of planting, each tree possesses supernatural properties. As a consequence, a drop of blood, which effectively is blood-coloured sap, can be taken from any of those special yew trees and used as an ingredient in magical potions, such as the poison potion needed to kill King Offalmire.' He then took out a small rolled parchment tied with a black ribbon from his robe, and handed it to Sylvia.

'Guard this parchment well lest it fall into the wrong hands, for without this, the list of what you need for the poison potion ingredients, your efforts will be futile and the task you have been charged with will fail.

'The list contains all of and the only ingredients you will need. You will have to collect all of them to enable you to make the magical killing potion. But it is paramount, as I have said, that the poison penetrates the eye of Offalmire on the tip of an arrow fashioned from the timber of, and shot from, a long bow which must also have been formed from one of the supernaturally blessed yew trees found in the grounds of Bowtown Hall. Nothing else will work!'

There is no other combination of ingredients or method strong enough or lethally capable of ridding the world of the evil King Offalmire. I wish you well in what could sometimes prove to be a perilous endeavour. Oh, and yes,' he paused, 'a very Happy Birthday to both of you!' He then disappeared......

Chapter Twelve

THE POISON LIST

'That really was brillfanmagical,' David said, as they set off after meeting Merlin. 'Who would have thought we would ever be able to actually meet Merlin the Magician?'

'The real Merlin,' Mary said. 'I like him, he's nice isn't he?'

'We were really honoured today,' Bill said, then turning to Sylvia, 'I'm glad we were right about him being here in this region. I wonder what he meant when he said it didn't happen last year?'

'I fancy some fish and chips,' David said, as the aroma of a chippy drifted in through the car window just as they were about to leave Bronzeford.

'Oh! Yes please. Me too,' agreed Mary.

'Okay. I'll find somewhere to pull up and park, and we'll get some,' Bill said.

'We've got drinks in the black bag,' Sylvia said, 'so we'll be all right with those.' With that, they parked in a side road, wound the windows down, and enjoyed some fish and chips.

'Can we have a look at what Merlin gave you, Mum?' Mary asked.

'Yes,' David said excitedly, 'let's see how we're supposed to poison old Offalmire.'

'Hold it there for a minute young man!' Bill said. 'I think you need to treat this a lot more seriously than that.'

David apologised and Sylvia, having first wiped her hands on a tissue, took the rolled parchment from the safety of her zipped bum bag.

At that moment a traffic warden knelt by Bill's open window. 'Excuse me, sir,' he said, 'there will be a large load coming down....' But that was as far as he got, as another warden at Sylvia's open window, shot his arm into the car and attempted to grab the parchment, but Sylvia was too quick for him. With a swift upward movement of her arm, she was able to smack the warden's wrist up against the roof of the car. Squealing with pain he pulled himself away as Bill started the engine and in seconds they sped off, leaving the bogus traffic wardens behind.

'That was a near thing,' Sylvia said, returning the parchment to the safety of her bum bag and zipping it. 'It would have been disastrous if they'd managed to get it. It's obvious **they** are everywhere. Sadly they can take any form that suits them. We'll have to try, if it's possible, to be even more careful from now on.'

'Perhaps Mary and I can create some kind of barrier round us?' David found himself suggesting, a big smile on his face.

Mary, continuing in the same vein of thinking, said, 'Something like a magical shield would do the job, Mum, don't you think? David and I think that we can do it, don't we, Bruv?'

David smiled and nodded, 'Yes, I think we can. Well, we can certainly give it a try. And I really dig this telepathy we can do now.'

'What a good idea you two. Well done! Let's hope you can create something like that. A safety barrier around the car would just the job,' Sylvia replied.

'There's a quiet bit of beach at Peg Dyke Sands,' Bill said, 'and it's possible to park next to the beach. We can then look at the parchment in safety. It's a place where a dyke comes out of a wide pipe on to the beach. Your mum and I had some fun playing a game in it when we were on our honeymoon. We used scallop seashells as little boats and raced them in the water running down the sand to the sea. It'll be a great place to sit and have a look at what we need to collect on the list of the poison ingredients.'

'Will we be able to have a go with the shells, Dad?' Mary and David together asked. 'It sounds like a lot of fun.'

Bill replied and continued, 'Yes, I'm sure we can. I think we could all do with a bit of proper relaxation, and yes, it will be fun! We should be there in about half an hour.'

Shortly after leaving Bronzeford, Bill suggested a slight change in the plan. They would first call in at a little village called Amberbeach which was also on the coast, as there were a few gift shops there in which they might like to browse. He also mentioned the interesting rocks on the beach and the entrances in the cliffs to old mines, some of which now formed caves.

'That sounds like a great place to explore,' Mary excitedly remarked.

'Yes,' David said agreeing with his sister, 'it sounds really interesting. So we will be going on a beach then? Great!'

Sylvia followed on with, 'And if I remember correctly, there's also a convenient public toilet there, which I'm sure we'll all find *convenient* before we leave.'

But the trip to the beach sadly didn't happen, for just as they were about to descend the steps towards the sands, Sylvia spotted a short and weird looking female. A woman who could easily pass for a witch had scuttled round a rock just off to their right and only seconds after David had said he thought he had detected an entity.

'I think we'd better postpone going to the beach here until another day,' Bill said. 'We don't want any more problems at the moment.' So they continued on to Peg Dyke Sands.

'You were right, Dad, it is a lovely beach,' Mary said, as Sylvia, who had driven from Amberbeach, drove off the road and parked their car at the top of the pebbled beachhead facing the sea in an area created for parking.

'Shall I look for some flattish sea shells or some small pieces of wood we can float?' David asked.

'No, not just yet, Son,' replied Bill. 'We must have a look at the parchment first. We've no idea, apart from some badger hair which your mum has, what we're going to need.'

'Okay, Dad,' David replied. He then grabbed Mary's hand, seemingly now knowing what to do and they both drew an imaginary circle around the car. A faint and transparent pale blue wall of light then magically appeared, totally enveloping it. The twins had created a protective shield.

'It's wonderful,' Mary announced excitedly. 'We did it! It's our first real piece of magic. I think I'm going to enjoy being a Terrestrial Twin. Well, some of the time.'

Sylvia addressing the twins then and said, 'And I want no, **no** interruptions. Okay?'

Sylvia, was now feeling totally safe as there was no one around and their car was enclosed within a protective shield. She again took out the parchment from the safety of her zipped bum bag and after removing the black ribbon slowly and carefully unwrapped it.

The whole parchment had a warm glow to it and was emitting a sort of pleasant humming sound. Then as Sylvia began to read, Merlin's voice took over......

Here is the list; you will need them all,
With a yew tree arrow Offalmire will fall.

He then continued through the list of items.

Poison Potion to Kill King Offalmire

I	*Hair of Badger*
II	*Mistletoe of Oak marinated in Leek Broth*
III	*Venom of Viper*
IV	*Droppings of Bat*
V	*Droppings of a Red Dragon*
VI	*A Drop of Two Virgins' Blood*
VII	*Terrestrial Twins' Water*
VIII	*A Drop of Blood from a Sacred Yew Tree*
IX	*A drop of St. Morn's Well water*
X	*Mud from King Offalmire's Lair*
	Stir well with wooden 'Love Spoon'

The twins' mouths simply dropped open with surprise at the next piece of information.

THE TWO VIRGINS' CHANT

To be chanted naked three times round the prepared potion
To fight and defeat King Offalmire's power
Mix the potion before second sixth hour
In Terrestrial Twins' Water must bubble this spell
Speak naught to no one lest they leave and tell
The Yew Tree Arrow flies to Offalmire's eye
With Terrestrial Light, evil Offalmire will die.

Form the killing bow and arrow from timber of the Sacred Yew Trees found only at Bowtown Hall.

It was all too much for David. He had to say something. 'Viper's venom, bat droppings,' he started.

Mary continued. 'Virgin's blood, Terrestrial Twins' water?'

'How on earth?' David interrupted. 'It's a hell of a list, Dad! Mum! Can we get all of them?'

Bill replied, 'We have to, Son. We don't really have a choice. By the sound of it some of them won't be easy, but we will have to somehow get them, all of them.'

'Won't be easy!' interrupted David. 'Nigh on impossible, don't you mean?'

Their mum joined in the conversation as she safely zipped the parchment back into the pocket of her bum bag. 'Look, we have Merlin's list which we have to complete, so we've got to work out how and from where we can get them all. As your dad said, we really don't have a choice, we need them. All of them! And we **will** get them all!'

David again joked. 'Blood from two virgins! I think that should be...' He looked at Mary and then at his parents before continuing. 'Well, I know I'm a virgin...' Mary tried to slap his face but missed.

'That wasn't funny, David! Not funny at all,' his mum said. 'Now apologise to your sister, and don't let me ever hear you talk like that again.'

David apologised, but his sister looked embarrassed and hurt. David then spoke again in a not very amused tone. 'And as for dancing naked...'

Mary joined in. 'I'm not doing that either!'

'We'll talk about it when we have to,' replied their mum. 'Let's first of all consider some of what's on the list.'

Addressing Bill, Sylvia then smilingly said, 'Do you remember when we joined the Rambler's Group, love? We once walked on the Castershire Coastal Path from

Scour Bay to Peg Dyke Sands. That walk took us past the entrances to one or two old mine workings. They were all sealed with bars, but I remember there were colonies of bats living in them.'

She now sounded excited. 'Well, we're in Peg Dyke Sands now. So the old mines are along there.' She pointed at the base of the cliffs. 'The entrances to the mines are only a few hundred yards away from where we are now actually standing.'

'But we still won't be able to get in,' David said.

'We'll think of something,' Mary added.

'If we are unsuccessful here,' Sylvia said, 'there are some caves at the far side of Scour Bay we could visit, and they also have bats in them.'

'I know,' Bill said, 'we'll have some fun on the beach for a while racing the floating shells and then eat our picnic tea. After that, we can walk to Scour Bay and the harbour. Perhaps have a boat trip. So there's a good chance the bats will be on the move in the evening when we come back.'

David interrupted, 'And I can ask them for some droppings,' he said cheerfully. They all laughed and went to look for suitable scallop shells.

It was great fun racing the shells and bits of driftwood in the dyke's water running down the beach, and as they had needed some relaxation all the family thoroughly enjoyed having some fun playing together.

Later, after finishing their picnic teas, they enjoyed the pleasant walk along the coastal path to Scour Bay......

But the list of items for the poison potion was nagging at each of their minds. As much as they knew they were supposed to, would they really be able to get **all** of them?

Chapter Thirteen

COLLECTING INGREDIENTS

The boat trip they decided to go out on after arriving at Scour Bay harbour was both surprisingly and frighteningly eventful. The scary action started shortly after they had left the harbour in the motorboat they hired. David had been trailing his hand in the water when something suddenly grabbed his arm and almost pulled him out of the boat. He tried to pull free but wasn't strong enough, as the Octifish, for that is what it was, was extremely heavy and had a firm grip on his right wrist.

Fortunately for David, he wasn't gripped by its mouth but by one of its eight eel-like arms. Mary tried to come to his rescue, doing her best to pull him free. But together, and even with their mum and dad's help, they were fighting a losing battle and the Octifish took a better hold, grabbing on to David's arm. He was in real danger of being pulled out of the boat into the sea.

'Can't you put a charge of electricity or something through your arm,' his dad suggested, 'I doubt it will like that.'

'You're probably right, Dad, I haven't got round to thinking about my new powers yet, but I'll give it a try.'

As Mary was still holding on to her brother, it meant the electric shock was twice as powerful and worked a treat. They all then got a good view of the Octifish as it reared and heaved its huge and terrifying green scaled body almost totally out of the sea. But it still had a firm grip on David's arm. Fortunately, the second shock wave they were able to send through it did the trick. After first shuddering for a few seconds, it started disintegrating as it began to slowly submerge, leaving David with a sore, very wet and slimy arm, but still safe in the boat.

Everyone was pleased and relieved when they finally reached the safety of the harbour and were once more on dry land, and it wasn't long before they were heading back to Peg Dyke Sands retracing their steps along the coastal path.

'We'll definitely have to try and be extra careful near water, Sis.' David said in a serious tone. 'We've been warned about water witches a couple of times now, and both of us have experienced real problems when we were wet, or even over water. We'll just have to try to keep dry from now on.'

Having retraced their steps along the coastal path and having almost reached Peg Dyke Sands, they arrived at the point where the sealed-off mine entrances were located. As Bill had anticipated, the bats had become active and were flying out through the metal grills sealing the entrances of the old mines to search for their evening meals.

'What's the plan then, you two?' their mum asked. 'How do you suggest we collect some......some bat droppings?'

David, looking around, picked up a discarded crisp bag. 'This will do,' he said, 'we'll simply ask the bats to help us.' He then held the bag close to a mine entrance and shouted in through the grill. **'Please Mister and Missus bats, can you help us?'** We need to collect some bat droppings.'

'Don't say why,' commented Mary.

'I wasn't going to,' replied David indignantly.

It was as if the bats were aware of exactly what the twins wanted and why, for only seconds later seven flew out of the mine together. They then totally amazed all the Knight family as they virtually lined up then hovered, one at a time, depositing what David had asked for in the crisps bag before flying off to find their suppers.

'Wow!' Mary said, 'I never expected that.'

Bill commented, 'I don't think any of us did, love.'

But he had no time to say anything else for another bat, larger than the first ones appeared hovering above them. Suddenly and terrifyingly quickly it grew to an enormous size, almost as big as their car. It then grabbed hold of both twins and after roughly pulling them up with its claw-like feet, it headed out to sea at high speed. Bill and Sylvia watched helplessly as it disappeared into the dim light. For a few seconds all that remained visible of the twins were their four legs helplessly kicking before they disappeared out of sight.

On the beach Bill picked up the crisp packet that David had dropped as he'd been plucked from the sand. Sylvia, terrified and understandably virtually screaming, ran to grasp his hand. '**Bill! Bill!** What can we do? Can we do anything?'

Bill felt totally hopeless. 'No, love, I don't think so. I honestly don't think we can,' he said as he put his arms round his wife in an attempt to comfort her. 'We can't even phone anyone for help....What could we tell them?'

'But will their magic still work over or in water?' Sylvia asked nervously.

'To be honest, love, again I really don't know. David said only half an hour ago that water might be a problem to them and I have a nasty feeling their powers might only work or work fully on land, or at least when they're dry.'

Having flown about a mile out to sea, the red-eyed monstrous bat gave out a hideous laugh and let go of its load, then simply disappeared, and down like helpless stones the twins plunged into the cold sea.

David grabbed Mary's hand as they surfaced, coughing and spitting water. 'Are you all right, Sis?' he nervously asked.

'I think so, Bruv, are you?' He nodded, spitting out more water.

'I feel as though our special powers have short-circuited in the sea,' he said, once his mouth was empty.

'We're both strong swimmers though,' Mary said. 'We'll just have to swim back to the beach.'

'We can try,' David said, 'but the tide is going out. It's going to be tricky, but we won't know if we don't try. We certainly can't stay out here.'

They both then became surprised and astonished as suddenly two dolphins and two porpoises surfaced in front of them. The nearest dolphin surprised them even more when it commenced speaking. 'Hardly a time to go swimming, you two, we'd better get you both back to dry land safe and sound.' Then, addressing one of the porpoises, it went on to say, 'You nip back first and let their parents know they are all right and what's happening, they'll be frightened to death with worry.' The porpoise having nodded quickly swam off and the dolphin spoke again. 'If you both open your legs, we'll come up underneath and give you a ride back, if that's all right?'

'I'll say!' the twins said together. 'It's more than all right, thank you.' Then off they went. As the fish were fast swimmers, it didn't take long to cover the mile back to where their upset parents were anxiously waiting.

'**Mary, David!**' Sylvia shouted as they stepped off the dolphins. 'Thank God you are both all right. We were so frightened. We just didn't know what was happening.'

'They did it for us,' David said, as he turned round. 'They saved us,' and addressing the dolphins said, 'Thank you!'

'Yes,' Mary said, 'thank you so much for saving us.'

'If we can't help the Terrestrial Twins, knowing what you two might have to face, who can we help?' the dolphin said. The dolphins and porpoises then all waved their tails and were gone.

Sylvia pulled both twins to her, giving them a big hug. 'I really thought we'd lost you that time.' And turning to her husband she said, 'Can it get any worse, Bill?'

'All I can say is, I hope not, love,' Bill replied. 'The trouble is we just don't know when, where or how they will strike. We have all been very careful, so I don't know how we can really do any more, but we need to keep going. Let's get you two back to the car, you must be frozen.'

'No, surprisingly I'm not, Mum, but I never thought I'd ever ride on the back of a dolphin,' David said.

'Me neither,' replied Mary. 'The ride was great, just great. In fact, cool! Well, perhaps a bit too cool!'

'It was brillfanmagical,' David continued, 'simply 'brillfanmagical.'

Then turning to Bill, 'Did you pick up the crisps bag, Dad? We're going to need that.'

'Yes I most certainly did. No need to worry, Son, it's too much important to lose now.'

No sooner had he finished speaking than a red-eyed bat with a round body about the size of a football shot between them, attempting to snatch the crisp bag. By expertly twisting himself and the bag out of its flight path and with a well-aimed, very hard kick, Bill sent the flying entity smashing into the cliff face, leaving an unsightly patch of green and brown runny mucus.

'Good kick, Dad,' David said. 'I think you scored a goal with that one.'

'Quickly,' Mum then said, 'let's run and get in the car now before there are any more problems. We can all certainly do without any more tonight.'

As they were only a couple of hundred yards from the car, it didn't take long for them to reach it. Once seated and belted-up, David said, 'Let's put another barrier on the car. That will help ensure we have a safe ride back.' They did, and also magically dried themselves as Sylvia drove them back to their holiday cottage.

David went to his bedroom, allowing Mary to have first use of the bathroom. Bill, addressing his wife, said, 'That's a birthday they're not going to forget in a hurry, are they, Sylv'?'

His wife replied, 'You're right there, love. No other teenagers have ever had a fifteenth birthday anything nearly as eventful as theirs has been!'

Bill finished with, 'Thankfully as they are both very much alive and still with us, I think we can now honestly say that it was a bit different and a very memorable and special day.'

Sylvia found a bucket under the sink into which the bat droppings and badger hair, having been popped into a sandwich bag, were both safely placed.

Having joined their parents in the kitchen, David and Mary were then happily able to make the first special items they had collected for the potion ingredients become invisible. They also made the parchment invisible after putting it in a Pringles container, which was then placed amongst the packets of biscuits in the kitchen cupboard. Everyone was pleased that the twins were now starting to get a grip on some of their newly acquired abilities.

David stuck his head round Mary's bedroom door when they were retiring for the night and said, 'I wonder what tomorrow has in store for us, Sis?'

'Not now, Bruv! No more for now if you don't mind! Just say goodnight and let's try to sleep on it...... Goodnight!'

'Good night, Sis, sweet dreams,' was David's parting, partially sarcastic reply.......But what might tomorrow have in store for them?

Chapter Fourteen

VENOM & LILYMIRE

Following breakfast and after the twins had washed the pots, Bill sensibly copied on to a piece of note paper the list of ingredients they needed to collect to make the potion with which to kill King Offalmire. By doing so, he was able to fold it and put it in any of his pockets having decided to not wear his bum bag. The original list presented to them by Merlin was again invisibly hidden and the Pringles package containing the special parchment was again concealed amongst the biscuits in the kitchen cupboard.

Bill then started the conversation saying, 'As I said yesterday, we need to determine which of the ingredients items can most easily be collected, so we can hopefully get them first. That will allow us more time to concentrate our efforts on acquiring the remainder and more difficult ones. So, where are we? What do we have so far?'

'Merlin gave us a tuft of badger hair,' Sylvia said.

'And we got the bat droppings last night,' David added.

Addressing the twins, Sylvia continued, 'Your blood and water won't be a problem.' The twins looked at each other and just shrugged their shoulders.

Bill followed with, 'And that I believe is it for now, two ingredients plus two available ones.'

'That means counting the yew tree bow and arrow as one, we need seven more plus a wooden love spoon,' Mary said. 'So which do we go for next?'

Bill replied, 'I've been thinking about number two on the list, the mistletoe. Why not ask the magpies in the garden if they can find some mistletoe for us and bring us a sprig.'

'That's a really cool idea, Dad,' David said, 'they're bound to know where some is growing.'

'But it has to be growing on an oak tree,' his mum reminded him.

'Right,' Mary said, 'come on, David, we'll go and ask the magpies now.'

Sure enough, as they had been since they arrived at the holiday cottage, the seven magical magpies were as usual roosting in the garden.

'I feel a lot safer when they are about, David, don't you?'

David nodding said, 'Yes, Sis, I do. We know they are supernatural ones here to help protect and possibly advise us. But like you say, they do help to make us feel more at ease.'

The twins then having first created a magical balloon encapsulating the magpies and themselves, just to be on the safe side, spoke to them.

'Good morning magpies,' both Mary and David found themselves saying together.

'Good morning Terrestrial Twins,' they replied in harmony.

'I think you are aware we have to collect a list of ingredients,' David said.

'And if it's possible, we need your help please,' continued Mary.

'Yes,' David said, 'we need a sprig of mistletoe, but it must have been growing on an oak tree. Could some of your group please be kind enough to help and find some for us?'

Both twins were delighted when without any hesitation seven magpies nodded and together said, 'Yes, no problem, we would love to.' The seven magpies then magically merged into one bird, which shot off like a fireworks rocket.

Back in the cottage, Sylvia was putting the picnic tea she had prepared earlier into their ever useful black carry-all bag. They all looked smart even though they were casually dressed. As usual they were wearing their black outfits of shorts, polo shirts and black and white trainers, and all except Bill were wearing their bum bags round their waists which they all found so useful, and which like their shirts and caps also displayed their Seven Magpies logo.

'Viper's venom is next,' Bill said. 'Vipers, as we all know are adders. So your mum and I have agreed to revisit the sand dunes at Serpent Dunes Sands to see if we can find some.'

David jumped in quickly with, 'But isn't that where the brakes failed and we went flying, Dad? Literally!'

'Yes, you're right, Son, it was,' Bill replied, 'but if you two put a magical shield on the car, it shouldn't happen again.'

The twins agreed they would, and did. Then they loaded all their bits and pieces and set off into another beautiful sunny Castershire June morning.

This time they arrived safely at the Serpent Dunes Sands beach, and again parked in the car park. Bill then surprised the twins with a branch he had taken from a tree in the garden. He had stripped it of its smaller branches leaving a two-pronged 'V' shape at the end. He informed them it was a snake-stick. It would be useful to pin down and hold an adder still when one was located, enabling them to be able to safely milk some venom from it. A small plastic ice cream cup he had picked up the night before was to be the container in which they would store the venom. Sylvia had also come up with the idea of sealing it with some cling film from the kitchen.

'That snake-stick is a great idea, Dad,' David said, 'have you ever caught any adders before?'

'Not since I was about your age, Son,' Bill replied, 'it should prove very interesting, but we will have to tread carefully. Not because of any danger from the adders, but we don't want to scare away any that we might come across. I can assure you they really are more scared of us than we need to be of them. Humans are rarely bitten.'

Having all visited the car park loo, they set off on their adder-hunting trip.

Using the end of his snake-stick Bill was able to show them what the snake's tracks might look like in the sand. Sure enough, after about twenty minutes of hunting, Mary spotted an adder basking in the sun. It was curled up in the sand dunes next to the road.

'Well done,' Bill said. 'That's a fully grown adder. So let's all be very quiet and careful and I'll see if I can pin it down.'

He then stealthily crept towards the snake, his forked stick poised ready for action. He had almost reached it when, with its beady red eyes now flashing, it suddenly grew to twice its size and tried to bite him as he came within striking distance. Only Bill's skill and quick reflexes saved him from the snake's fangs. However, the snake growing in size and attacking Bill was only the first surprise. The second came from Mary, who was now nearest to the creature. She suddenly began mumbling words that no one could understand and at the same time pointed her forefinger at the snake. As she did a jagged shimmering light, rather like a bolt of thin lightning, shot from the end of her finger striking the snake just behind its head. And to the delight of everyone, particularly Mary, it quivered for a couple of seconds, stiffened and froze where it was.

'I just seemed to know what to do and say,' she said.

'Well, whatever it was you said it did the trick. Well done!' Bill said, as he grasped the now immobile adder just behind its head where Mary had zapped it.

Sylvia passed him the ice cream carton from their black bag and by using the edge of the carton Bill forced the snake's mouth open. He then, by applying pressure on its fangs, was able to milk venom straight from its teeth into the carton.

Sylvia then wrapped a piece of cling film over the carton, having earlier cleverly stuck some round the side of a drinks bottle for transporting. Next, a strip of sticky tape from a pocket size dispenser she had found in the cottage's Welsh dresser, effectively secured the carton's valuable contents. The snake then returned to normal size and they let it wriggle away.

'I never thought we'd ever go snake hunting,' David said when they returned to the car.

'No. It's a bit different,' Sylvia said. 'But we knew this holiday was going to be.....well, different.'

'It's brillfanmagical,' David said, 'and it looks like we might be getting an idea of how to use some of our magical abilities, especially if what Mary did with the snake is anything to go by. So where are we off to next, Dad?'

'We're on our way to a place called Lilymire, Son. There's a great walk which takes us round a lake and it's a pleasant walk of which your mum and I are very fond. The lake's often covered with water lilies and is a really tranquil and peaceful place. According to many, but not all scholars, it is also thought to possibly be the lake, and one of the many, into which King Arthur's sword *Excalibur* might have been cast after the Battle of Cammlan.'

'Cool,' replied David.

'So your dad has again applied his favourite "Don't Know" formula, and thinks this lake is probably the one.' The twins, aware of their dad's 'Don't Know' formula, just grinned.

'Is there anything else special round here to see, Dad?' asked Mary.

Sylvia replied, 'Yes, love, there are a number, but the one I think you and David would most probably like to see, and which we can visit after lunch, is an unusual place known as Lilymire Grotto, or as it's sometimes called, Lilymire Abbey.'

'What's that? David asked turning towards his mum.

'Yes, David, I feel it too,' Mary said, 'what is Lilymire Grotto? It feels like it's important.'

'Well, from what I remember,' Sylvia said, 'it's the site of some sort of ancient building containing a labyrinth of caverns and tunnels. I believe it was created, and that's a good way of describing it, in the fifth or sixth century. But some scholars think it was much earlier. The front of it was cleverly hewn from the face of what is believed to have been a quarry.

'It is thought that those working in the quarry came across the entrances to virtually a warren of caves, and that an imaginative locally powerful person decided to take advantage of them. Some think he may have been guided by an outside source as to how and why he built it. But no one really knows. But by adding to, shaping and modifying what naturally was there, someone was able to create a special sort of place. And believe me, it really is different.'

Bill then joined in. 'No one thinks it ever was an abbey, but that it earned that title over the many years it was in use. Possibly because for some reason, and no one knows why, many locally important people were buried in it. It was also reputed to be a site regularly visited by the Knights of the Round Table. Some of them may have been laid to rest there. No one knows.'

'What I do know is that it has been of interest to the druids for centuries, and there are many recorded sightings of creatures and entities. There have even been some of a paranormal nature, and those have been of considerable interest to ufo'ologists since the fifties, particularly because of its design, as it is so similar to buildings on the other side of the world. How on earth, and from where and how did those who built it get their ideas? Some think from extraterrestrials.'

'Over the years there have been a number of times that sightseers have got lost in its maze of catacomb type tunnels. Some were missing for more than a day, and oddly when they emerged they had no recollection of being lost or of ever having being in there.'

'That was of particular concern to their families and friends,' Sylvia said, 'but also to official departments because the rooves of some caves are said to be unsafe. Or so they say!'

'Wow!' was the joint sound which came from the twins.

'It sounds a terrific place, Mum,' David said, and Mary most definitely agreed.

Bill then took over the conversation. 'Some folklore writings also say that one person who may be buried there could be Sir Gawain, a famous Arthurian knight. According to some legendary writings, he was King Arthur's favourite and most successful knight, and the one who was at the side of Arthur when he died. Some mythological scripts also say that Sir Gawain spent the remainder of his life in an enclosed place after King Arthur's death, and a number consider Lilymire Grotto could possibly be the location.'

'You can imagine your dad has also applied his favourite "Don't Know" formula to all those folklore ideas too,' Sylvia said. 'And as a consequence, we have always thought it made a lot of sense, especially as it is also thought that Sir Gawain possibly was the knight who threw the sword *Excalibur* into the lake. As we know one of the lakes on the list is Lilymire Lake, which is less than two miles from the grotto, it makes a lot of sense that both locations are probably the places mentioned in the various recorded versions of mythology and folklore. To us it makes an awful lot of sense, and it's not by coincidence Lilymire Lake is the place we are shortly going to visit. Let's hope we don't have any problems there......'

Chapter Fifteen

LILYMIRE LAKE

The journey to Lilymire village was fortunately uneventful, and Bill drove to the lake.

'We'll use the lake's own car park,' Bill said. 'We can walk around the lake first and then go into the village for lunch. We will also take you to have a look at Lilymire Grotto. Okay?'

'Sounds like a good plan to me,' Mary said.

'Are there any fish in the ponds, Dad?' David asked.

'Yes, Son, in fact they are regularly fished by the locals for silver fish. There are big pike and some huge eels in there too. It's a perfect lake for eels being so near to the sea.'

'The lake is shaped something like a figure of eight with an island in the centre,' Sylvia said, having picked up on the conversation, 'which can be reached in two places by wooden walkways, one on either side. The platforms allow visitors to cross the lake at its narrowest points. By then using the steps and footpath it's possible to go up and over the hill to the other side. There's also a multi-arched old bridge across the wider part of the lake.'

David suddenly grasped Mary's hand and they stopped.

'What's the matter?' asked their mum, tension showing in her voice.

Bill also asked, 'Is something wrong?'

'I'm not sure what it is,' replied David, 'but there is a feeling...' He paused, 'A feeling of foreboding here. It's something...something sinister, somewhere near here.'

'I can feel it too,' Mary said. 'We're not that close to it yet. But whatever it is, it's not far away, and it isn't nice!'

'I mentioned earlier,' Bill said, 'that this is one of the lakes into which Arthur's sword *Excalibur* was possibly thrown after the battle in which he died. Well, these waters are also listed as possibly one of the likely waters from which the Lady of the Lake produced the sword in the first place. Could it be something connected to her that is giving you the feeling?'

'We don't really know, Dad,' Mary replied. 'But whatever it is, it just doesn't feel right. To be honest, it feels evil. Very evil!'

With that they proceeded to cross over on the wooden walkway towards the island. They were less than halfway across when it happened!

Two huge slimy eels shot up and out from the water. One grabbed hold of David's right ankle; the other grabbed one of Mary's. As the twins were gripping each other's hands while they crossed over the lake on the very narrow walkway, twinning, they were able to point at the eels with their free hands and simultaneously fire at them. Just like before, when Mary had fired a thin bolt of lightning at the adder, the reaction was immediate. The eels instantly let go their grip, straightened and shuddered. But this time the results were different. They dissolved into sausage-like strings of slimy mucus before disappearing below the surface, both having been grabbed by a pair of large hungry pike.

Having assured their parents they were both all right, they continued across the lake and up to the top of the hill.

The higher position gave them an excellent view of much of the lake and they all commented on how attractive the lilies looked. But the twins were now feeling more than a little uneasy.

'There is still something else,' David said, 'and it's not far away, and it really isn't very nice. Do you feel it, Sis?'

'Yes, Bruv, I do. Whatever it is, and as nasty as those eels were, they aren't what I am sensing now. This is a lot nastier, and as I said earlier, whatever it is it's fiendishly evil.'

Having carefully descended the path and steps at the far side of the hill, and as they were about to step on to the other wooden walkway, a pair of swans gliding majestically across the surface of the lake gracefully swam towards them.

'Aren't they lovely,' Mary said.

'Beautiful and majestic,' replied her mum.

Mary then asked, 'Remind me, Dad. How can I tell which is which. Which is the male and which is the female swan?'

Bill replied, 'The one with the slightly larger dark bump on its beak, between its eyes, is the cob, the male. The other is his mate. She's called a pen.'

At that moment, the female swan stopped moving and after seemingly standing on the water and having twice flapped her wings shocked them all when she suddenly and in a flash of shimmering pink light transformed into an attractive lady about as old as their mum and wearing a long white cotton dress. Her blonde hair fell over her shoulders to her waist.

Speaking in a soft pleasant voice she said, 'I am sorry if I startled you. But I did not want to miss the opportunity of speaking with you. I know who **you** are. Allow me to introduce myself. You may have heard of me, for over the centuries and in many legends and folklore writings I have often been referred to as the Lady of the Lake.'

There were gasps from both Mary and her mum, and David grabbed Mary's hand, gripping it tightly. Both of them had suddenly felt very, very uneasy. A threat was beaming at their minds from the lake, and they didn't like it, not one bit.

'My partner and I,' the swan lady continued, 'are aware you are experiencing a few problems, and as we are both able to magically change shape, we thought we might offer you our services. We can help you find the hidden Crystal Tower.'

'THAT'S IT, THAT'S ENOUGH!' David angrily shouted. 'IN FACT IT'S MORE THAN ENOUGH. NO MORE! It's not help you two are offering, it's interference. You just want to find out where the Crystal Tower is and what we are planning!'

Mary then continued, 'You don't really want to help us at all! In fact quite the opposite! You just want to use us to get at the Crystal Tower's secrets!'

Their mum looked particularly shocked at their seemingly unprovoked outburst. But then she suddenly grabbed Bill's arm and stepped back in shock as the white lady in a puff of green and brown smoke suddenly again totally changed her appearance. She now looked awful. She had become a hunchbacked and unbelievably badly wrinkled, ugly old hag with long, straight and greasy grey hair, and was now wearing a dirty brown cloak over a very soiled sack cloth smock. She now looked a disgusting picture of evil!

At the same time the cob swan disappeared as it dived below the surface of the lake through a mass of erupting bubbles. Then, and for only a brief second or two, it showed the awesome sight of what looked rather like a scaly and hairy grey backside as it disgustingly farted as it submerged. All that was left was a revolting patch of smelly green mucus floating on the surface of the lake.

Not wanting to hang about any longer, the twins simultaneously enveloped their parents with their free arms and loudly said, '**Back to the car!**' And sure enough, as quick as a wink, they were all seated in relevant safety having returned to their car.

'What on earth was all that about?' Sylvia said, turning to the twins with a shocked expression on her face.

'I think I know,' Bill said. 'She was the mythical Lady of the Lake and...'

Mary interrupted, 'And...and who, Dad, who, what?'

I think you know who,' David said joining in. 'It was Offalmire. King Offalmire. He knows the whereabouts of the Lady of the Lake and that the sword *Excalibur* may have been thrown into this lake.'

Interrupting, Bill said, 'He's possibly been searching for it, intending to use it against you two.'

'Let's hope he doesn't find it then,' Sylvia said. 'That sword could prove to be a very powerful weapon if it was ever used against any of us.'

'But one good thing did come out of what happened,' Bill said. 'I am sure that was Offalmire. And if it was, we now know where his lair probably is. Looking at the map before we set off reminded me of the multi-arched bridge which is situated a little further up the lake, and as he is half troll, under one of the arches would be an ideal place for him to live.' The twins, looking at each other, agreed.

David then said, 'Yes, Dad. We both agree with you, but what about that magical ride back to the car. Now that really was brillfanmagical, wasn't it?'

'It most certainly was,' his mum replied. 'That's another powerful and useful ability to add to your growing list. But now I think it's time for something to eat. Let's go for some lunch.' So they left their car in the lake's car park and walked the short distance into the village.

'Her face was really awful. I wonder why she was so terribly wrinkled?' Mary asked, thinking of the hag's gross appearance.

'That's easy,' David jokingly replied, 'would you ever enjoy having to try to iron your face if it was as wrinkled as that.'

Then, holding hands, they all walked into the village laughing......but wondering what the afternoon might bring.......

Chapter Sixteen

LILYMIRE GROTTO

During lunch it was agreed that as both their parents had said so much about the site known as Lilymire Grotto, and the twins had experienced such strange vibes about it, going to have a look at the structure seemed inevitable. So Bill drove to the car park on the edge of what looked like it might at sometime have been a quarry in which the complex had been created.

'Wow! What a weird looking place,' Mary said, looking perplexed.

'You can say that again,' David said.

'Wow! What a weird...' Mary jokingly started to say when David interrupted her saying, 'Okay, Sis, I asked for that.'

'Yes, Bruv, you really did. But it is weird isn't it? I think we can honestly say it's different, very different!' Having paused to have a slightly longer look at the structure that had been built on to and out from the face of the quarry wall, she continued. 'I really wouldn't ever have expected to see a building that looks like this built into the side of a quarry, and certainly not such a building of this design in this country. It's got a row of eight Roman type pillars along the front and it's topped with a structure similar to that of the Parthenon in Athens. How weird is that? '

'And what about those castellated half round towers at either end,' David said. 'You're right, Sis, it really does look weird. It's totally out of place. The building, or what we can see as the front of the structure, looks to be about a hundred or so feet long and about sixty or seventy feet high, but the entrance through that open archway is around thirty feet from the ground. And oddly there are no steps up to it. How on earth did anyone ever get into the place?'

'I can answer that for you, Son,' Bill said. 'There used to be an impressive flight of stairs flanked by stone sculptures of animals and other creatures, but the stairs were removed by the local council in an attempt to keep people out. It's considered to be dangerous because of possible roof falls. Look, there are "DANGER KEEP OUT" notices everywhere.'

'You two can explore the place on your own if you want to while your dad and I lay in the sun,' Sylvia said. 'We can keep an eye on you from up here. But please, please be careful.'

'We will, Mum,' came back the obvious reply from both of them as the twins slowly walked down the sloping track that led to the front of the structure.

Having stopped at the spot where the stairs would have started, they both experienced a strange tingling sensation, and they instinctively twinned, tightly grasping each other's hand.

'Somebody or something is trying to contact us, Sis,' David said, 'or I think they are.'

'And you know I can sense it too, Bruv,' was Mary's reply. 'So, what do you think we should do about it?'

'It is certainly coming out of the grotto,' was David's reply, 'do you fancy going in?'

'I don't see why not. If we don't, we'll always wonder who or what it was trying to contact us.'

'I totally agree with you, Sis. As we're holding hands,

twinning, let's fly up and into that arched entrance.' Microseconds later they were in.

'Right, we made it. So what can we see?'

'Very little, Bruv, as there isn't much light getting in through those narrow windows.'

'No, apart from the light entering through this arched doorway, it's all pretty dim.'

David had barely finished speaking when two torches, one either side of the door, suddenly and surprisingly burst into flame, and for a moment or two dumbfounded the twins.

'Well, it looks like somebody or something expects us to use these torches and explore,' David said with a noticeable tone of apprehension in his voice. 'Shall we?'

'I'm game if you are, Bruv, but need I say, we'll have to be on our toes. Let's not forget we're here in Castershire to get rid of King Offalmire, so we don't want to put ourselves in any situation where he might be able to get rid of us.'

As she finished speaking they were both again taken by surprise. A big badger suddenly lumbered out of a hole in the wall and after first standing erect, it spoke. 'Good afternoon twins, we hope you are enjoying your holiday. I have a message for you from Merlin. He says, because you were influenced to come into the grotto, he thinks, but isn't entirely sure, that maybe the person who enticed you in was Sir Gawain. He is one of the many special people interred in this complex and because he is aware of your task, and how dangerous it might be, he has offered his services. All you need to do is to ask for him.' And with that the badger disappeared.

'Can you believe it, Bruv? Sir Gawain is buried here, and wants to be in our team.'

Mary had barely finished requesting Sir Gawain to join them, than amazing things started to happen. The twins marvelled as the passage they were standing in took on an eerie pale golden glow. The strongest beam of the light first slowly and spookily moved up and around the passage and then from one wall to the other. After moving up to the ceiling, it then crept down the wall behind them and only stopped moving when it reached a place on the floor between them.

Having become motionless, the strange glow creepily changed into a shimmering pale blue light which slowly rose to slightly higher than David's head, then stopped. Then they watched in total amazement as a tall figure began to slowly materialize between them and continued to do so until a handsome young man, wonderfully dressed in a magnificent suit of light armour, stood between them in the now fading blue beam.

The twins were gob-smacked, totally flabbergasted! The knight then amazed them even more when he spoke. 'I thank you so much for inviting me to join you. I was aware that the task given to you possibly might be a very dangerous one, therefore I communicated through Merlin to the Gods of the Terrestrial Light to offer my services. I was delighted when I sensed you felt I might be of assistance. Again pretty maiden,' he took Mary's hand and kissed the back of it, 'again I thank you. No matter what, if I can ever be of service to you, I would deem it an honour. I am, as you know, Sir Gawain. I retired to this place after King Arthur's death, and was eventually interred here.'

He then took a closer look at the Seven Magpies logo on David's shirt and cap.

'I see you both wear the coat of arms of a knight, but I do not recall ever seeing a coat of arms such as yours.'

David straightened up and proudly said, 'Allow me to present ourselves to you, sir. This pretty young lady,' he said, smiling at his sister, 'is my twin sister, Mary. I, sir, am David. Our powerful father is William Knight and our attractive mother is known as Sylvia Knight.'

'You truly are Knights,' Sir Gawain said. 'But are you the Terrestrial Twins we have all been eagerly awaiting? I thought you were coming last year, but I obviously got that wrong.'

'Yes,' Mary said with pride. 'Yes, we are the Terrestrial Twins and oddly enough, that's the second time we have heard that we were expected last year.'

Having heard they were indeed the Terrestrial Twins, the knight stepped one pace back and bowed low to them, which made the twins glow with both embarrassment and pride.

'I was grateful you called for and asked to see me, but could I be so bold as to enquire if I might be permitted to join you in your battle against the evil black side of magic, against those from the Other Side? It is such a long time since I enjoyed a good fight. As I have said, I would deem it both a favour and an honour. But only if I may be of service to you.'

'We think it's a fantastic idea,' the twins said together.

David then continued. 'We would be honoured to have you on our side, Sir Gawain. To have you fighting with us would certainly strengthen our Knights' team, and thank you for enticing us into this grotto.'

The twins both smiled at what Sir Gawain said next. 'I really would like to be in your team, count me in! All you need to do when you want me is to simply call my name or think you need me and I'll be there. But before I go, I have to tell you I was not the one who enticed you in.' He again bowed, smiled and faded away.

As Sir Gawain disappeared, so too did the remains of the golden glow which had illuminated the stone passageway while he was with them. Then, amazingly, just as the light finally faded, the twins were astounded as they were somehow suddenly transported from where they had been standing into a corridor whose walls, ceiling and floor had the appearance of polished aluminium. Not only did the fabric of their surroundings appear to be metallic, every surface was radiating a pale glow of purple light. David and Mary were then shocked and dismayed to discover that they both had lost control of their bodies and so were unable to do anything to prevent what was happening to them. The twins no longer felt apprehensive; now they felt horrifically and unmercifully trapped!

Chapter Seventeen

ABDUCTED!

Then a horrendous thing happened that justified David and Mary's sense of feeling totally trapped! Even before they had a chance to think or telepathically communicate with each other, let alone speak, they both were totally soaked by a fine spray of ice cold water which assaulted them from every direction from hundreds of small concealed water jets. There was no way of escaping the power-draining drenching to which they both were now so terrifyingly being subjected. All they could do was to stand still and aimlessly hold hands. Whatever strengths and powers they had, were gone... They both now sadly were totally at the mercy of their abductor.

Then, just as fast as the water jets had started spraying, they stopped. At the same time, the purple light which somehow had now totally enveloped them, dimmed as the water drained away and simply disappeared. The twins sadly looked and felt like cold, drowned rats.

David was the first to speak, but wasn't really sure of what to say. 'Are you all right, Sis?' he found himself saying.

'As well as might be expected, Bruv, I think. How about you? But what the hell was all that about?'

'I'm not sure, Sis. But who or whatever it was that was responsible, certainly knew how to knock our supernatural abilities into touch. I'm sure that like you, Mary, I'm that wet and cold I just can't stop shivering. Let's hug and see if that helps,' and they both put their arms round each other for a loving hug in an attempt to feel warmer.

The twins' actions seemingly prompted a response from some dark shadowy figures which had appeared literally out of the wall. But it was impossible to really see who or what they were as the low purple illumination had become even dimmer. David and Mary then became aware that they had been lifted from the base of the metal corridor and were now being transported about a foot from the floor by some sort of tractor beam. And they didn't like it one bit. Where on earth was it taking them? Who was doing it, and why?

Their mental questions were soon unpleasantly answered as the realization dawned fearfully on them that, as sad and frightening as it was, they had now totally lost all control of their own bodies. Although they could still see and hear, they couldn't move a muscle. David and Mary were again unfortunately entirely at the mercy of their captor or captors.

They then were parted from each other before being unceremoniously totally undressed and then laid on to separate shiny metal tables, which thankfully were quite warm. From what they could see of the room into which they had been transported it could best be described as a well-equipped operating theatre with brilliant spotlights illuminating every part of their bodies. Were they really still in the grotto, or had they been transported out and beamed somewhere else?

The twins occasionally, but only briefly, caught sight of their abductors. They looked like little grey figures with inverted turnip-shaped heads and two large pale green eyes. They kept touching, pressing, exploring and examining every fraction of the twins' bodies. Sometimes with their scrawny little hands, other times gently and carefully with instruments and probes as they slowly moved round them. But thankfully they didn't hurt either of them.

Their captors' actions and the whole situation made David and Mary think their experience was rather like the 1947 Roswell Incident in New Mexico that they had read about and researched on the net, but in reverse. Both twins felt that they were or had been in the presence of extraterrestrials.

Suddenly, or so it seemed, it was all over, and David and Mary found themselves, fully dressed, flying down and out through the entrance to the grotto. As they landed, they almost knocked over their mum and dad who had been looking out for them.

'Thank God you're all right,' Sylvia said in what was obviously a very concerned voice, 'you've finally come out. Your dad and I have been frantic with worry. You've been in there over two and a half hours. What on earth have you been doing?' And she caringly grabbed their hands and gave them a combined big motherly hug.

'Yes,' Bill said, 'what on earth have you been up to, your mum's been very upset? Did you get lost in there or something?'

'Let's just get back to the car first, please, Dad?' David said. 'We are both in need of a sit down. Perhaps then we can relax a bit and tell you all about it.'

To say Bill and Sylvia were shocked and astounded by the twins' explanation of their absence would be a gross understatement. They were totally amazed. Gob-smacked!

'Were they aliens then, extraterrestrials?' Sylvia found herself asking. 'Did they hurt you, either of you, especially you, Mary? You know what I mean?'

'No, Mum, they didn't, Mary replied, 'they just examined me.' And being kind and thoughtful of her mum, she continued, 'it was okay. It was just like being examined by our own doctor. But we can only guess as to who and what they were. Thankfully they weren't any of Offalmire's cronies.'

David managed to defuse the obvious tense situation by making light of what had been a very frightening experience saying, 'I wonder how much my wrinkly bits weighed?'

But before their mum could jump in with an expected comment, Mary quickly said, 'And what about us meeting Sir Gawain then. He is buried in there and wants to be part of our team against Offalmire. What do think about that, Mum? You'll love him. I know you will. I think he's wonderful.'

'Did he really offer to join us?' Bill asked.

'He most certainly did,' David replied. Then he totally amazed his parents when he followed on by asking, 'Would you like to meet him?'

Sylvia even surprised herself by being first to quickly answer with, 'If we can, I would love to meet him!'

Bill followed on with, 'Yes, Son, I don't see why not.'

The twins asked their parents to get out of the car with them, and as they stood together grasping each other's hands they were relieved to realize that their bodies were now back to normal. With a huge smile on her face Mary said, 'If you are free to join us, Sir Gawain, please do.' And to everyone's satisfaction, he did.

Again Sir Gawain materialized in all his splendour. 'That was quick,' he said, having immediately appeared. 'I thought it would possibly be a longer time before you again called me, but I am proud to be at you service.' This time it was Bill and Sylvia's turn to look amazed.

The twins enjoyed introducing Sir Gawain to their mum and dad, having first thanked him for arriving so promptly. They all talked generally for a couple of minutes or so about King Offalmire and his goblins, and about the importance of the coming big event. Then, after again saying, 'Call me or think about me if I am needed and I will be there,' Sir Gawain smiled, bowed and having kissed the back of both Mary's and Sylvia's hands, simply faded away.

'He seems a really nice guy,' Bill said.

'Oh yes, he most certainly is!' Sylvia said, with a big grin on her face.

Bill then continued, 'He could prove to be very helpful. I hope we don't have one, but if we do have a big fight, it would be great to have him on our side.'

After getting back into their car Bill said, 'Your mum and I have been thinking. We need to develop a plan, but first we have to find out where the Crystal Tower is really situated. It's supposed to be on an island, a little way off the coast. But your mum and I feel it is somewhere closer. Perhaps we might talk about it later.'

'Okay, Dad,' David said, 'it's fine by Mary and me,' he added, sensing what his sister was feeling, 'but I have to say, and it's for both of us, that Sis and I feel that Lilymire Grotto is an incredible place. Even considering all that happened, it really got to us and I reckon one day we'll both be back.'

Bill then changed the subject, 'While you were away, I had a thought.'

'Really, Dad?' David exclaimed, but said no more.

'Yes, Son, I did, but not about you two.' Both David and Mary pretended to look hurt.

Ignoring their twisted humour, their dad continued. 'St. Crane's Minster is a wonderful building and as we need to be in that area for one of the ingredients, I suggest if we have time that we consider going there before we have some tea.'

Everyone agreed, so off they went.

Their route was to take them back into and through the town of Moatcaster, but just before they reached it Sylvia suggested a change of plan. As it was a fair distance to St. Crane's from where they were, and as the twins' abduction had taken up most of the afternoon, she decided it would make more sense if they stopped in Moatcaster to do a little shopping. Their St. Crane's outing could wait until tomorrow.

'I need to get some bits and pieces from the supermarket, particularly milk and some spray cream just in case we need them. We also need to buy a suitable pan or container in which to mix and boil the ingredients for the poison. And apart from that, we need some groceries. I still have to feed you. So, what I am suggesting is that Mary and I go shopping. You, David, can go with your dad to have a look for that concealed end of the old latrine chute at the rear of the castle below the King's Banqueting Hall that your dad was talking about on the way here. It will give both of you something to do.'

'Good idea, love,' Bill said, 'and if I'm right, and it does still exist, it comes out at the base of the wall on which Moatcaster Castle sits. It could possibly be hidden by rocks and gorse bushes. Well, it was when I was your age, kids. It's just off the path that runs down the side of the river moat. Yes, it is a good idea, love and will give both of us something to do.'

'You're going to have to get out a bit more often, Dad,' David joked, 'if looking for a shi...' he stopped just in time, 'if looking for a latrine chute is your idea of fun!'

Fortunately everyone saw the funny side of his comment and laughed.

Bill was lucky enough to find a place to park at the rear of the castle and they all set off to do their thing, Sylvia shopping with Mary, Bill and David in search of the end of the latrine chute. And David was still chuckling to himself.

'It's here, Dad,' declared David, having gone a little way ahead and having scrambled over some rocks and forced his way between a couple of gorse bushes. 'It's definitely sealed up. Just look at those steel bars round the bottom of the chute. No one could ever get in there, even if they wanted to!'

'I'm not so sure,' Bill replied. 'If you were very small, you could easily slip through the bars of the grill.'

'Ah! I see what you mean,' replied David, jokingly continuing, 'I'll bear that in mind if I ever want to go up.'

They both walked a little further along the footpath alongside the river. Bill informed David that before the weir had been built about a hundred years ago about half a mile downstream, boats had travelled up from the sea. They had loaded and unloaded all sorts of things in a small harbour which had been situated just before the arched bridge as the river was conveniently about fifty yards wide at that point. Bill also pointed out where another latrine chute and a wider chute from the kitchen below the King's Banqueting Hall emerged from the castle. Chutes which had allowed the kitchen and latrine waste to shoot out and hopefully into the river to be washed out to sea.

'It must have stunk rotten in those days, Dad,' David said. 'I wouldn't have enjoyed a walk down here then, as I am sure a lot of the, let's call it *waste*, wouldn't have actually reached the river!'

They were just about to return to the car and passing the first chute which David had found a little earlier when a voice they instantly recognised as that of the red dragon amazingly echoed out of the chute. 'Good afternoon, gentlemen,' it started, 'I didn't expect to hear your voices for at least a couple of days.'

Both Bill and David spoke their 'hellos' through the bars and up the chute.

David then continued, 'What do you mean, you didn't expect to see us for at least a couple of days?'

'Well,' the dragon said, 'you are collecting the ingredients for the poison at the moment, aren't you?'

'Yes,' David replied, 'we most certainly are.'

'That means you are unable to make the poison yet, doesn't it?' continued the dragon. 'So you won't be able to complete your task for at least a couple of days.'

'Why "a couple of days" though, and why here again?' David asked in a puzzled voice.

The dragon replied, 'Well, unless I have got things wrong, or am speaking out of turn, you will be coming here to try and finish off King Offalmire. Won't you?'

Bill came into the conversation at this point. 'Let's just forget the couple of days for a minute, dragon. Why are you expecting it to happen here, here at Moatcaster Castle?'

'That's easy,' the dragon replied. 'This is where Merlin really hid the Crystal Tower. It's here. It's hidden here inside the King's Tower. It's invisible, like me, but I can assure you, this is where it is. I am the guardian of the Crystal Tower.'

He paused, and Bill and David turned to look at each other and to absorb what they had just heard. Dragon then continued, 'Oops, it is obvious from the surprised look on both your faces, I can see you down the chute you know, that you were not aware of those facts. I hope I am not going to get into trouble. Merlin said it was a secret but I thought you knew all about it.'

David then picked up the conversation. 'Both Mary and I felt there was something special about the King's Tower. I said it was brillfanmagical, and now we know it really is.'

'And so do those two little horrors,' Bill said, as two little goblins who had been hiding at the base of the chute came scuttling out, transforming into rats before diving into the river.

'Offalmire also will now know where it is,' David said. 'We should have known King Offalmire would have had someone watching our every move. Now that he knows, or will shortly know, it means he too will probably need a couple of days to prepare an attack to get into the King's Tower.'

'I told you I didn't expect you for a couple of days, as that was what Merlin had said. So that means it has all been cleverly planned by him, now I don't feel so bad.'

'One of the ingredients we have yet to collect is some red dragon droppings,' David said addressing the dragon. 'Could you please drop some in the garden when you're out flying tonight?'

'It will be my pleasure to be of assistance, David.'

David then asked the dragon, 'Will it be all right if we call you "Red" from now on, rather than just dragon, dragon?'

The dragon thought for a moment or two, and then happily replied, 'Yes, I would like that very much. After all, I am a red dragon. Yes, I will enjoy being called Red. Thank you!'

As Bill and David returned to their car, David started to giggle and said, 'I'm sorry, Dad, but I've got to say it.'

'Say what?' questioned Bill.

'With Red calling on us tonight, that really does mean we're going to be dumped on from a great height!'

Though a little annoyed at David's words, Bill couldn't help appreciating his son's humour and laughed with him......

But Bill's thoughts were elsewhere. He couldn't help thinking about what still needed to be done for their encounter with King Offalmire.

Two more days; and what else might happen......?

Chapter Eighteen

ANOTHER EVENTFUL DAY

David and his dad reached their car as Mary and her mum were crossing the road.

'That was a good bit of timing,' Sylvia said who, like Mary, was carrying a shopping bag in each hand. 'Let's get these into the car and find a quiet place to have our picnic tea. Oh and yes, I bought some leeks for the *you know what*.'

David was bursting to tell them what Red had said but his father had told him to say nothing. Bill's finger held up against his lips was message enough for now.

'There's a nice picnic area and a great beach to explore at a place called Tollvale,' Bill said as he drove out of the town. 'The castle there has been used in lots of films and television series, but we'll just enjoy our picnic on the beach and do a bit of exploring. We can visit the castle another day.'

'That sounds all right to me,' Mary said.

'Me too,' said David, 'but we'd better watch out for any more problems.'

Having found a suitable spot at the head of the beach they started unpacking their tea.

'It's a lovely looking castle,' Sylvia said, 'it really is worth a visit. Your father and I spent quite a bit of time walking and exploring the woods, beaches and caves in the area.'

'Caves,' jumped in Mary, 'proper caves?'

That was too much for David. He had done well to keep quiet as instructed by his father, but the mention of caves was too much. He excitedly turned to Bill.

'Let me tell them about this afternoon and talking to the dragon up the chute at King's Banqueting Hall, Dad. Please!'

'Okay, Son,' smiled Bill, 'but take your time.'

'It's in Moatcaster Castle,' he blurted out.

'At the beginning, Son,' Bill said, 'start at the beginning.'

David then went on to tell his mum and sister what had happened and what the dragon had said and that dragon is now called Red. His words giving all the facts and detail were greeted by looks of disbelief on the faces of both of them. Mary was first to speak.

'We said there was something special about the King's Tower. We could feel it. But we never thought the Crystal Tower Merlin had hid was inside it. But, as it's invisible, how on earth could we have known?'

David continued, 'We couldn't, Sis. We'd an idea there was something very special about it, but there is no way we could have guessed about the Crystal Tower being in there. We just had a feeling of... just a supernatural magical feeling. But while we're talking about the Crystal Tower, I have to tell you Mum and Dad that Mary and I have been telepathically communicating with each other since we left Lilymire Grotto. We're not quite sure how we feel about our experience, and wanted to put a few things to you.'

Sylvia came in straight away with, 'We can understand you both would be having thoughts about your abduction, for that's obviously what it was, but...'

Bill then came in saying, 'Let's first listen to what they have to say, love, before we start forming opinions. Go ahead, you two, let's hear what you've been thinking about.'

Mary started, 'David and I have been weighing up everything in our minds, as we have since been able to recollect just about everything that happened to us and possibly what the strange experience was all about.'

David came in at this point saying, 'We really don't want to alarm either of you, but we feel you need to know everything that happened, just in case you feel some of it affects or might affect some of our plans.'

Mary continued, 'The most important thing is that we weren't harmed in any way. Who or whatever they were certainly could have killed us if they had wanted to, but as they didn't, that proves they were not linked to King Offalmire, which has got to be a good thing.'

'But,' David said, 'apart from fully examining our bodies, they also examined our brains, having placed probes in our ears and noses, and metal caps of some sort on our heads.'

'But they didn't hurt us,' Mary said, 'they were extremely careful.'

'All of which,' David said, 'brings us to a number of questions. Did they know who we were, the Terrestrial Twins etc, or did they simply examine us because we are twins, which makes us different to singular individuals?'

'Or,' Mary said, 'did they examine us to find out about our new powers?'

'Or,' David said, 'do they have a hidden agenda? Are they possibly also interested in stealing the special hidden treasures for their own possibly devious use, and so tried to find out what we knew?'

'Or,' Mary said, attempting to defuse the strained expression developing on her mum's face, 'was it because we had been daft enough to allow ourselves to be enticed into the grotto in the first place?'

'Well,' their dad said, 'your little brains have been busy communicating with each other, haven't they? This is what I think. It now really does appear that you both experienced an extraterrestrial encounter. They cleverly enticed you into the grotto because they knew who you were. They simply took advantage of the opportunity your presence presented to them. If I had been an alien and was presented with such a fantastic opportunity as you two literally arriving on my doorstep, I would have abducted you as well.

'As for any hidden agendas, we'll just have to wait and see. What matters is that they didn't harm you. Neither of you seem any worse off from your experience, so we thank God for that.' And he took Sylvia in his arms and gave her a special loving hug.

'Now don't go all soppy on us you two,' David joked.

'Yes it's like your father said,' Sylvia added, 'the most important thing is that you are both okay. As for the other stuff, I think it's a *watch this space* sort of situation.'

When Bill went back to the car for a bag they had left, David went with him and said, 'I don't know about you, Dad, but me and Mary have also been thinking about for how long those aliens might have been in those catacombs? It could have been for centuries or even many thousands of years. And what might be on their agenda? Not only that, how many more similar places might there be in the country, or how many could there be round the world where extraterrestrials are based?'

'I only wish I could answer your questions, Son, but sadly I can't. But please don't ask your mum. I really do think as things are she already has enough on her mind.'

'Okay, Dad, I won't. But I think Mary and I will be visiting Lillymire Grotto on another occasion.'

'I think we should all now try and quieten down for a little while and have some tea,' Sylvia said when they were all seated together. 'Later we can explore round the beach and rock pools and just think things out a little bit more. It's another popular surfing beach. Perhaps we can watch the surfers for a time.'

As usual everyone enjoyed Sylvia's picnic tea, and seemed to heed her advice. In fact the whole family was particularly quiet and thoughtful, but the idea of exploring the rock pools was something the twins couldn't resist, so they went off with their dad leaving poor mum to tidy up as usual.

Splashing just a drop of water onto David, Mary said, 'I think these are the best rock pools we've ever found. There are crabs and fish here as well as little creepy crawlies.'

But the peacefulness of the warm and pleasant afternoon was suddenly shattered, for after having sensed a reason for looking back to where his mum was, David suddenly shouted in horror. 'DAD! MARY! MUM'S BEING ATTACKED!'

Both Bill and Mary looked up to see Sylvia, who now had a bin liner over her head and shoulders, with her legs kicking, being dragged off by two long haired characters in brown one-piece overalls.

'GRAB MARY'S HAND, DAD!' David yelled, as he took hold of his dad's other hand. 'Let's see again how powerful our magic can be.' Having said that he shouted, 'FLY US TO RESCUE MUM!'

Their feet lifted simultaneously and at what seemed like fifty miles per hour they shot off the rocks and flew across the beach looking rather like a multi-fuselaged airplane to where their mum was struggling against her assailants.

Bill's well-aimed feet landed with a bang in the middle of the back of one of the attackers at the same time as David's feet crashed into the back of the head of the other. Their fighting skills were then properly tested for the first time when, and after having rescued Sylvia from her captors, David and his father found themselves literally fighting for their own lives.

Whoever or whatever their attackers were, they certainly knew how to fight. Each of them in turn went through a variety of vigorous swings, punches, chops and kicks. Bill, having eventually knocked out his attacker, helped David to floor his aggressor with a sharp blow to the side of his neck and the fight was over.

When Sylvia's attackers had to finally accept defeat, they transformed into red-eyed rats. But before they could escape, David and his sister zapped them and watched them melt into the usual pool of snotty, muddy mucus. Meanwhile, Mary had taken off the bin liner from around her mum, having first had the difficult task of removing the magic rope with which it had been secured.

'I never really saw them,' Sylvia breathlessly stated. 'They appeared out of nowhere, and after the bag had been pulled over my head that magical rope twirled around me preventing me from doing anything. I had no idea what was happening. Thank you for spotting I was in trouble and for coming so quickly to my rescue.' She then gave them all a big 'thank you' kiss.

'Are you sure you're okay, love?' Bill asked a notably concerned tone in his voice.

'Yes, I'm fine, Bill really, thank you! But I'll feel a lot safer when we get back to the cottage.' She had obviously been shaken by the event.

As everyone sensibly agreed, they quickly packed up everything and drove back to their holiday base.

'Oh look!' Mary said as they disembarked from the car. 'The magpies have brought us some mistletoe!'

'Thank you magpies,' they all said, and picked it up from the doorstep where it had been left.

David, giggling to himself said, 'Red said he would be dropping something for us tonight. So don't go into the garden after dark!'

'And that's quite enough on that subject, David, thank you,' his dad said, 'there's no need to say any more.' Knowing only too well what he meant they all laughed and went into the cottage.

Once inside, David made the bucket reappear and put the newly acquired ingredients in. He then returned it to its invisible state. Just before they went to bed he then surprised everyone by saying, 'Do you fancy having a fly over the fields and round the cottage before we go to bed, Sis?'

Mary looked gob-smacked for a second, but smilingly replied, 'What a cool idea, Bruv. I'd almost forgotten we flew out in the open, or sort of, for the first time today. Yes, it's a great idea, let's go and enjoy it.'

'Be careful,' Sylvia said, as they walked out into the garden, gripping each other's hands. 'Don't go far.'

'We won't, Mum,' David replied as their feet lifted off the ground and they swooped up to steadily fly round the cottage and the garden.

Before returning to terra firma, they flew over to glance down at the cow pasture and the little wood in which the magpies liked to spend time. Their parents simply watched with glowing admiration.

'Now that's a proper way to finish a day,' Bill said, after the twins had landed and as they turned to go back into the cottage grinning from ear to ear. Bill was last to enter and as he did there was a dull thud and a splattering sound behind him that made him jump. A smile then spread across his face as he quietly closed the door...Red, as promised, had made his deposit!

But was tomorrow going to put smiles on their faces?

Chapter Nineteen

ST. CRANE'S & MORE INGREDIENTS

The first day of collecting some of the ingredients with which to make the poison to kill Offalmire had been a mixture of magical happenings and a spot of tourism. However, the next day for collecting more ingredients started much earlier than was planned, in fact at about half past one in the morning.

Bill, having been disturbed by the sound of both twins leaving their bedrooms, followed by the sound of the back door opening, woke Sylvia. They both quickly went outside and were shocked and terrified to observe both David and Mary, still in there night gear, about to jump down the well which was situated in the corner of the garden.

Fortunately their parents managed to grab and hold on to both of the twins just after they had swung their legs over the side of the well, meaning to drop themselves down.

'They're fast asleep!' Sylvia whispered to Bill. 'They're both sleepwalking,' she said as she slowly led the way, gently guiding and returning the snoozing Mary back into the cottage. Bill carefully followed-on behind guiding David. It was obvious neither of the twins had any idea of what was happening to them or what they had tried to do.

Once indoors, the twins were carefully escorted back to bed. **Something** had somehow managed to make them sleepwalk, almost to their deaths in the well. Was it to be another eventful day?

'I think we'll have to take it in turns to sleep,' Bill said. 'Three hours on and off, to make sure it doesn't happen again. I'll sit in the lounge first, love. You go back to bed.'

As Sylvia was too tired to argue, she did what Bill had suggested, having first given him a kiss on the cheek. It was only when she woke in the morning that Sylvia realized Bill hadn't disturb her and fortunately the rest of the night had been uneventful.

After breakfast, and having said nothing to the twins about their sleepwalking episode, they set off on a very hot morning for St. Crane's Minster.

'We have to go over that Devil's Valley Bridge again don't we?' Mary questioned nervously.

'No,' her dad replied. 'If we first go slightly north, we can head straight for Morndale which is where St. Crane's is. By going that way, we won't go anywhere near the bridge.'

'Let's go that way then please, Dad,' David said, having now joined in. 'I would hate to have to go over that bridge in daylight. Red wouldn't be around to give us a lift if we needed one, if you know what I mean, would he?'

'Okay,' Sylvia replied. 'So that's the way we'll go.'

'It's fine by me,' Bill joked, 'I'm just the chauffeur!'

'Wasn't it Morndale where you were born, Dad?' Mary asked.

'No, love, but it wasn't that far from there, near the old harbour outside Moatcaster.'

'And I was born in Moatcaster,' Sylvia said, 'not far away from the harbour. But we can visit them both another day.'

'And I was born in bed, cos I wanted to be near my mum,' David jokingly said, and they all enjoyed the quip.

They had decided to leave Red's deposit where it had landed until their return, as no one wanted to mess up the usual favourite black strip they were wearing and spoil what was developing into a really beautiful morning. The stench of dragon dung on them would have turned any day sour!

'St. Crane's Minster is a beautiful building,' Sylvia said, 'there are some magnificent tall pillars inside and for some reason I get a funny feeling every time I visit it.'

Bill found a suitable parking place on arrival in Morndale and they set off on foot to have a look round before visiting the Minster. They explored the centre of the town for a while including visiting the museum and the car boot sale in the old market place, but their minds wanted to be in the Minster, so that's where they next went.

Once inside, they entered the first of the magnificent oak pews and all knelt, bowing their heads in a short private prayer. As every other of the Minster's previous visitors had done before them, they too found they had difficulty in describing, even to themselves, the majesty and splendour of the masons' building talents and the skillful and picturesque craftsmanship contained within the walls in such a magnificent House of God.

They were silent as they reverently and slowly walked down the centre of the nave, gazing around in awe as they attempted to take in the whole majesty and splendid appearance formed by the huge columns and arches that reached up into the space high above them. Words were totally unnecessary. It would have been difficult to describe how much the quality of the Minster's carvings and ornate roof impressed them.

Shafts of glowing sunlight pierced the general gloom of the huge interior, illuminating everything they touched. In so doing, they created a welcoming air of loftiness and godliness. The impressive range of contrasting and changing shades of dark and light formed by the piercing almost searching beams of sunlight, some fading to create pale and dark shadows, gave the whole interior of the Minster a welcoming yet at the same time eerie appearance.

All the Knight family felt it had been a special and unforgettable experience and a privilege just to have visited such a wonderful place.

'From where are we going to collect the well water, Dad?' David asked as they returned to the car.

'We're going to an ancient well on the coast about a mile from here, Son. It actually overlooks what's called St. Morn's Bay. Legend has it that on the day St. Morn drowned during a raging storm a few miles out from here, a spring emerged from the rocks above the coast and its water is said to have magical properties. That is no doubt the reason why Merlin included it on his "you know what" list.'

'It's a nice little spot this is,' Sylvia said when they reached the well, 'and this is the first time any of us have visited here. I really like it, the whole area is so attractive. Views like these are what people expect of Castershire. It really is lovely…The scenery is absolutely stunning.'

'Has this vaulted stone arch that's covering the spring head and the well been here long, Dad, do you know?' was David's first question when they arrived at St. Morn's Well.

'I honestly don't know, Son,' Bill replied, 'but what I do think is that the one that we are now looking at probably isn't the original.'

Sylvia being the most organized and domesticated family member had washed out a small screw-topped drinks bottle ready to collect a sample of the well's water and passed it to Mary. 'Do we need a full bottle, Mum?' she asked.

'I shouldn't think so, love,' was Sylvia's reply, 'but thinking again, you had better fill it. Having to come all the way back to here if we spilled some and there wasn't enough left would be a little annoying to say the least. So yes, love, you had better fill the bottle.'

'It looks as though it could be a bit whiffy inside that arch, Sis,' David said, 'I think you'd do as well to scoop some up from that sunken pool area the spring water is running through before it falls through the grill covering the well rather than risk leaning into there.'

Mary agreed, but as she bent down, it happened. One of Offalmire's morons surprised everyone when having materialized out of thin air it leapt out from under the little arched vault, attempting to snatch the bottle from Mary with one hand while doing its best to thrust an evil looking triple-bladed knife into her with the other. The mistake it made was attempting to attack one of the Terrestrial Twins at all. It was a brave fighter though and tried hard to kill her; it even had a go at David when he joined in to assist his sister.

The fight moved out from the well after Mary, using some very clever twisting, kicking, thumping, parrying and acrobatic leaping moves, including virtually running up the wall displaying the well's information board, and springing back in an overhead cartwheel type movement to the other side, cleverly avoided the slashing blades. As the well was situated close to the top of the cliff, it wasn't long before the fight moved from within the confines of the spring and well to out near to the edge of the cliff, a perilous position in which to be fighting at all. But the entity, having been disarmed by David, was now fighting for its survival, and fought and kicked as best it could.

However, following a wrong move it made and a skillful kick from Mary when it took the fight back to her after David had lost his footing in yet another damned rabbit hole, she saw the end of the attack. Their assailant, having been skillfully kicked backwards, and accompanied by a terrified blood curdling scream, with its arms and legs wildly and helplessly thrashing the air disappeared from sight over the cliff edge.

Mary then nimbly jumped back into the edge of the well and having picked up the bottle she had earlier been attempting to fill before being interrupted said, and to the amusement of the other family members, 'Now, where was I?'

'Right,' Sylvia said in a superior voice after she just managed to safely secure the bottle full of well water in her Seven Magpies bum-bag which was firmly and safely fitted round her waist. 'I think that's it, and well done, you two! I'm glad you weren't wearing your caps today, or you might have lost them. Now we've got what we came for, I suggest we move on, just in case there are any more of Offalmire's warriors hanging about. Let's push on up the coast and find somewhere for lunch. We can then go on to...' she paused, 'to where we said we were going to go.'

They all smiled and Bill drove out of Morndale. The route he had chosen gave them an opportunity to enjoy some more of the attractive scenery for which Castershire is justly famous. The rugged coast was wonderful and greenery and hills dotted with trees afforded them some magnificent scenery, and there was an abundance of wild flowers and butterflies everywhere.

They had just started to ascend a reasonably steep hill when the tailgate of a trailer being towed by a tractor ahead of them burst its fasteners and dropped down. At the same time the two ropes securing two very large circular bales of hay snapped like gunshots. Bill now had a different sort of twin problem as both bales lurched off the trailer and came thundering down the hill, hurtling towards their car.

He swore under his breath, then loudly and calmly said, 'Oh dear, they're up to their tricks again,' as he swung the car across the road to avoid the first bale, then swung back to his own side of the road and braked, cleverly avoiding the second bale as they watched it too go thundering past. When they looked forward, both the tractor and its trailer had vanished, as had the two bales of hay.

Sylvia congratulated her husband on his terrific driving and for saving them yet again. Bill just smiled and shrugged his shoulders and they moved off to continue their journey.

'Where shall we stop for lunch, love?' Sylvia asked.

Bill surprised them with his answer. 'The Severed Head Inn in Fishington has some fantastically interesting ancient chairs and tables, and all sorts of armour on the walls and in its passageways, even in the toilets. As it's also about three quarters of the way to where we want to be next, it should be a great place in which to eat, so I suggest that's where we have lunch.'

'As long as there aren't any more cannons,' David said.

Mary then commented. 'It was in Fishington, wasn't it, Dad, where we were shot at in the harbour?'

'Yes, love, it was,' Sylvia said, 'and that really scared all of us, Mary, not just you!'

'Yes,' Bill said, 'that was an experience none of us are ever likely to forget, but we should be all right today.'

Chapter Twenty

THE BLEEDING TREE

Everyone had thought that having lunch in Fishington was an excellent idea but, sadly, all of them encountered problems when they went to use the loos before going into the dining area.Mary and her mum had just entered the ladies room, which fortunately was quite large, when they were astonished to find they were being attacked by someone or something in a full suit of light armour wielding a rapier sword. Both ladies jointly responded with flying kicks which sent their assailant crashing against the door of one of the cubicles which flew open, and the armour clad fighter fell in, literally. Sadly for it, it went head first into the toilet pan.

Mary immediately took advantage of their downed attacker when, after first having snatched a slender epée sword off the wall and having literally jumped onto the legs of their assailant, she meaningfully and powerfully thrust the sword up through a gap in between its back armour plate and the chain mail covering its rear, which had slipped down. The result was a bloodcurdling gurgling scream which emerged from within the armour as the whole of their attacker turned into a gooey, jelly-like grey and green mucus before disappearing down inside the toilet bowl, which Mary flushed.

'**You** can have that one, love,' Sylvia said smiling, 'I'll use the other cubicle if you don't mind.'

Meanwhile, in the corridor outside the gents, both Bill and David were also engaged in a real old battle, not with something in armour but with just a couple of rapier swords flashing around in thin air on their own. The lads, like Mary, also needed to snatch rapier swords off the wall with which to defend themselves.

'Open the door to the men's room,' David said to his dad, 'I have an idea.' Having opened the door and after they had fought the flashing swords into, then across the room, David suggested with a big grin on his face that they knock the swords that were attacking them down, to enable them to jam the points into one of the three urinals on the wall. And together they managed to do it. With their pointed ends now firmly wedged into the hole, all the two swords could do was to wiggle about. They were both desperately struggling but were not going anywhere. No way!

'It came to me while we were fighting, Dad. Twins water is a major ingredient in the poison to kill Offalmire, so if it will help kill him, it probably won't do these two swords a great deal of good either. We've nothing to lose by trying.'

His dad just looked on, amazed at the idea but said nothing as David tried his experiment. And it worked. No sooner had David finished, than the swords shuddered one more time, then having turned into a mucus-like pool of jelly, slowly slurped down through the hole in the bottom of the urinal and out of sight. David, grinning broadly, enjoyed the stunned expression on his father's face as he jokingly said, 'Just one wiz and they were gone!'

Having gone to the dining room to meet the other family members, they all enjoyed talking about their morning's experiences, but as David's dad had asked him not to divulge how he had got rid of the swords, and being a good son, he didn't...... Well, not until after lunch.

After they had enjoyed a good meal and returned to their car, Sylvia drove them to Bowtown Hall to get the next ingredient they needed for the poison potion.

The ruins of the old hall were a couple or so miles out of town and were not often visited by locals because of the ghost stories and strange happenings that occurred from time to time, so they had no problem parking outside the hall, or what was left of it. It was also a good spot close to the start of the avenue of the supernaturally blessed yew trees.

'Now, and before we go any further or do anything at all here at Bowtown Hall,' Bill said, 'you two will need to put a screen around us to prevent any of Offalmire's goblins, or any other of his entities, from hearing or seeing what we are doing. So, David and Mary, please do your thing!' And they did. They cleverly created a moving barrier around them making them all feel much safer.

'Didn't Merlin say there were fifty two of the yew trees?' David asked as they got out of their car.

'Yes, Son, he did,' Sylvia replied.

'And they go all the way up to what's left of an old summerhouse,' Mary said, 'and I fancy having a look at that.'

'It should be a nice walk too along the avenue,' Sylvia said. 'We can imagine ourselves as being the Bow Master's family walking up the avenue, which is what they must have done centuries ago.'

She had just finished speaking when the ghostly image of a headless horseman, wearing a smock shirt and brown trousers and riding a black horse, came thundering down the avenue straight at them. As all of them were extremely fit they had no problem avoiding the mounted ghost rider. However, they thought their car was going to be less fortunate as having slightly changed direction they helplessly watched as the horse continued its wild run, heading straight for their car. At the moment they expected to hear the crash, the ghost horse with glowing red eyes rode straight through it and out of the other side.

'That must be one of the apparitions the locals are afraid of,' Bill said., 'I wonder if there will be any more. But just in case we do get any problems, let's get on with what we came here for.'

'They really do look like they are bleeding,' Mary said, when they had a close look at one of the supernaturally blessed yew trees that had some of its bark slightly damaged and from which some sap was oozing.

'It's weird,' David said, 'have you brought one of those ice cream cartons in your bag to put some in, Mum?'

'Would I forget something so important?' Sylvia joked. 'Here we are. I'll use this bit of stick to scrape some in.'

'Now for the difficult one,' Bill said, 'the special bow and arrow. I know you two,' he gestured to the twins, 'have been whispering about something. So what is it that's so secretive that you have decided to do?'

'It's not really that clever, Dad,' replied David. 'Sir Gawain, like all knights, would have been an excellent archer. And as the longbow was developed in the area he used to be in, he would be an ideal person to make the bow and arrow for us. He's bound to be able to do a better job than we can. He will also be able to shoot the poisoned arrow at Offalmire's eye.' Everyone thought it was a great and sensible idea, so the twins called upon Sir Gawain to join them.

He arrived in an instant, the twins again introducing him to their parents who marvelled at his appearance. Sir Gawain had been quite a ladies' man in his day and having carefully taken hold of Sylvia's hand he gently kissed the back of it.

'Your knight,' he said, nodding towards Bill, 'is indeed a fortunate fellow. For you are truly a most beautiful lady. I am honoured once more to make your acquaintance,' and he bowed. 'Your every wish is my command.'

The twins looked like they were going to puke at such language…but didn't.

It was David who broke the embarrassing spell by asking his dad for the multi-bladed Swiss Army Knife he had brought for the occasion.

'This,' said David, opening the knife to the fine saw blade and offering it to Sir Gawain, 'is what you can use to cut the yew tree branches for the bow and arrows.'

But before he allowed the knight to start his task, David drew Sir Gawain to one side and whispered in his ear for a little over two minutes. Sir Gawain then said, 'You can now leave me in this supernaturally blessed place. I know what is required of me and will be ready to do battle when called.'

Turning to Bill he continued, 'May I keep this wonderful tool, sir? I believe it may prove to be very useful.'

'Yes, you can keep it,' Bill said, 'with my compliments!'

'I am honoured, sir,' was the knight's reply. 'And I thank you all of you for including me in this, your special destiny adventure.' He again bowed, faded and disappeared.

'Wow!' Sylvia joked, 'I don't think I'll ever wash that hand again. But that's two more important jobs completed.'

They enjoyed spending a little more time exploring the ruins and gardens of Bowtown Hall, and then decided it was time to be moving on.

'Time to get back I think,' Bill said, 'perhaps you two,' he looked across at the twins, 'might try to get a bit of shut-eye? I reckon your mum could do with a nap too.' So they belted up and set off to drive back to their holiday cottage.

They were about halfway back when Bill became aware of a police car with blue flashing lights and a blaring siren coming up fast behind him and he slowed down. The police car's loud hailer then blurted out for him to pull over and stop. So he did, about two thirds up a hill and the police car stopped behind them. The sirens and loud hailer noises had woken Sylvia and the twins who were now looking at Bill with puzzled expressions on their faces which prompted him to speak.

'Honest, I haven't done anything wrong. I wasn't speeding or anything. He just hailed me and asked me to stop.'

As David looked out of the rear window a shocked expression appeared on his face. At the same time the policeman now standing next to the car was asking Bill to lower his window when David yelled, 'DON'T, DAD! DON'T OPEN THE WINDOW!' and grabbing Mary's hand, used his forefinger to quickly trace a circle round the car shouting, 'PLEASE PROTECT US!'

Within the same second, the policeman amazed them all by pulling a sawn-off shotgun from behind his back and pointing it at the occupants of the car. Then, with a silly grin on his face, his evil eyes now glowing red, he simultaneously fired off both barrels of the gun.

The reaction was instantaneous. As the explosive sound echoed through their car, the pellets from both cartridges hit the magical shield the twins had created only a micro-second earlier.

As it all occurred so quickly it was difficult to clearly see what happened. But on impact all the pellets immediately rebounded from the force shield and shot up and backwards in the direction in which they had just come. The gun was caught in the reflected blast and now whirling dangerously hurtled back around decapitating the 'police' goblin. His hands and arms disintegrated by the pellets, his listless body then flopped down on to the road, his detached head rolling down the hill.

All four members of the Knight family were holding their ears which had suffered from the impact and vibration of the explosion and all wore painful grimaces on their faces. 'Thank you both!' Bill said, 'but how on earth did you know that something was wrong, David?'

'It was his car, Dad. Whoever prepared the car for him created a police car with the word "Garda" on it. That meant it was supposed to be an Irish police car. So, as I know we're in Castershire and nowhere near Ireland, I knew it was a fake.'

'Thank God you did, Son,' Sylva said, 'that would probably have been curtains for all of us. Thank you!'

When they looked round they found, not surprisingly, that the police car and rolling head were gone.

'I've got to say it, Dad,' David said grinning, 'he's now completely off his head and totally armless, and would you believe it, he also left empty handed!'

They all laughed, Bill then moved off continuing on the journey back to their holiday cottage.

'Oh no!' Sylvia said when she went into the garden, her remark bringing everyone running out and fearing the worst.

'We didn't check did we? But part of that deposit Red dropped for us last night splattered some of the washing hanging on the clothes line. Just look at the twins' shirts.'

'I told you we were going to get...' David started.

Before he could finish Bill interjected. 'Enough, David. Help your mum to clean them up a bit with the garden hose before she brings them in for washing.'

'For washing!' Mary blurted out. 'You don't think I'm going to wear it again, do you, Dad?' 'Me neither,' David said.

'You most certainly are,' replied Sylvia. 'You won't know it ever happened when they've been washed.'

'But, Mum,' Mary started.

'No "buts", Mary. They're going to be washed!'

David then brought in a bit of Red's gift in a plastic sandwich bag and put it in the bucket, muttering to himself.

'What a load of...'

Chapter Twenty One

ATTACKED FROM THE AIR

There were no nasty unwelcome surprises in the night, and everyone woke early to yet another beautiful day. Over breakfast, Bill suggested they go to the theme park which was only a few miles away. Having described some of the rides to them, the twins were bursting at the seams to go, not even arguing when asked to wash and wipe the breakfast dishes and put everything away.

'We can go there this morning,' he said. 'We'll stay for lunch and collect the rest of the things we want in Moatcaster before re-visiting Lilymire Lake. Hopefully this time we'll get some mud from Offalmire's lair.'

'That then should be almost everything we need to collect,' Sylvia said picking up on the conversation. 'With the mud and the twins' stuff, we'll be able to actually mix the poison potion when we get back.'

'Yes, you will need it tonight,' a voice from behind them said, making them all jump.

Sylvia spoke first. 'Oh! Merlin, you gave us all a scare. But it's good to see you. Good morning!'

Everyone else said the same and Merlin then continued, 'Dragon has informed me there's been a lot of activity round the King's Tower these last two evenings. This, I feel would have been Offalmire's goblins and other entities collecting information and doing a complete reconnoiter of the tower and the surrounding area. Doing so would help him to devise a plan…I only wish I knew what it was. Unfortunately, his powers have now become so strong they are preventing me from reading his thoughts. I am magically being blocked out and I don't like it.

'However, the Crystal Tower is still invisible and safely hidden in Moatcaster Castle's King's Tower. Fortunately for us Offalmire has no idea as yet of how to get into it to remove the Thirteen Treasures, or at least I don't think so. But this is the reason why you two, the Terrestrial Twins, are here to ensure he is defeated before he is able to get in. It is possible he now has developed almost enough power and knowledge to achieve his objective. But we will soon know. As for the present time, apart from me, you twins are the only ones who can enter the Crystal Tower.'

'But how can we?' David asked in a surprised voice.

'Because both of you are physical keys. Either of you can simply walk straight in at any time that you want.'

'But does Offalmire know that?' Bill enquired.

'No, I don't think so. Not yet. But then again he might.'

Bill continued, 'But that then places the twins in a very dangerous position, doesn't it, Merlin?'

'Possibly, Bill, but I have complete faith in their abilities and the power of the Gods of the Terrestrial Light,' replied Merlin. 'And let's not forget, I am not going to be very far away. Even though I am not always visible. I also understand you have enlisted the help of Sir Gawain, that was a splendid idea. He has the reputation of being a formidable fighter, so it is far better you have him on your side than as an opponent. I am sure he will be very useful.

'I will leave you now, but I will join you later on the eight-arched bridge over Lilymire Lake. We can then finalize our plans. But please get the mud you require before I arrive. By doing so, you will create an interest in what we are doing for the Other World entities to take note, and it is most important that we do…Oh! And enjoy your trip to the theme park.' He then disappeared.

The trip to the theme park was a huge success. The twins enjoyed the exciting and gut-wrenching experiences on all the big rides. They particularly enjoyed the ride that took them through and then high above the trees, even though they had to resort to zapping two swinging monkey-like goblins who tried very hard to throw them off at the very highest point of the ride. They all also enjoyed their lunches, even though Bill and Sylvia thought putting anything into their stomachs after some of those rides might have proved to be a bit foolhardy. But fortunately they didn't need to have been concerned.

'What a great place that park is,' David said, 'I'd gladly go there again.'

'Me too,' agreed Mary.

Bill then drove to and parked outside a supermarket in the Moatcaster retail park.

'I would like you two to go into that big general store over there,' their mum said. 'It's where Red lowered us into a car park after saving us from that horrible waterspout. We need a love spoon, some round balloons and at least a dozen small screw-top bottles of orange or something. You choose. It's the bottles your dad wants not what's in them, okay? Oh, and also a couple of small backpacks and a belt for each of you. If they don't have any belts, try and get some strong string instead.'

'Why balloons, Mum?' David asked.

'Yes, Mum,' continued Mary, 'why balloons? What are they going to be used for?'

'It's your dad who wants them, love. Apparently they are part of the plan, part of our strategy. He'll no doubt explain more fully when everything else is ready, so get what you can. We're going to the supermarket for some other things.'

'We'll talk about it all later,' Bill said with a big grin on his face.

'Don't you just hate it when Dad grins like that, Sis?' David remarked. 'I'm sure he's got something up his sleeve he's not telling us about.'

Mary jokingly replied as they went into the store, 'It's probably just his arm, Bruv!'

They all met back at the car as arranged. The twins, however, being the first back were pleasantly surprised to see seven magpies perched on it and both politely said, 'Hello.' David then enquired as to why they were paying them a visit.

'Is there a special reason for you all being here?' he asked, just as his mum and dad joined them laden down with shopping bags. 'Is there something we need to know?'

Mary then asked with tension in her voice, 'Are there some entities somewhere that you've come to warn us about? It's not Offalmire himself is it?'

'No, Mary,' the magpie perched above the driver's door said, 'there is no immediate danger, but there could be when you get to the bridge with eight arches at Lilymire Lake. We wanted to wish you good fortune in your mission and to let you know we won't be far away if we are needed. Oh, and to help you, the arch you want is the fifth arch from the Pebblequay end of the bridge.'

The family thanked the magpies for their kind thoughts and the information. The magpies having said 'Cheerio' simply vanished.

'That was good of the magpies to come and wish us good luck, wasn't it?' Sylvia said, 'I have always felt safer and happier since we first met them. It's always comforting to know they're not very far away. They have proved to be great guardians.'

'And I am sure we all agree with you, love,' Bill said. 'I'm sorry if we kept you both waiting, kids, but it was really busy in there. Did you manage to get everything?'

'Apart from belts or strong string,' Mary answered, 'but we decided we could use our own bum bags as we are usually wearing them. But we still don't know what everything is for?'

Their dad said he would tell them all about it later, but not now where they might be overheard as they didn't have a safety barrier round them. So they loaded everything into the car and set off to again visit Lilymire Lake.

'I didn't see a multi-arched bridge when we were here last time, Dad,' David said. 'Where is it?'

'It's a wonder we saw anything at all last time,' Bill jokingly replied. 'We were all a bit distracted for want of a better word by the Lady of the Lake and, what we think was Offalmire's revolting backside.' His last remark brought a giggle from the twins.

'If our walk hadn't been disrupted and shortened, we probably would have visited the bridge. It wasn't far from where we were last time, just a bit further inland towards the wider end of the lake. I'm heading for a quiet little village called Pebblequay now and we'll park there. We can explore the old quay first before walking to the bridge, it's not far. Hopefully we will then be able to get some mud from Offalmire's lair and with fingers crossed without any more problems before again meeting up with Merlin.'

Because they were both apprehensive and excited about again going to Lilymire Lake, and also about visiting the multi-arched bridge to retrieve some mud from where they hoped they would find Offalmire's lair, the twins quickly got bored with Pebblequay and asked if they could move on.

The sun was high in the sky and the temperature had risen to a little over 30 degrees when they reached the start of the bridge and they were all glad the way their caps shielded their eyes from the bright rays of the sun. David had to be different. He turned his cap for the peak to shade his neck.

Bill guessed the twins would have enjoyed having a swim as it had become so hot but he wasn't prepared to risk their lives by allowing them to swim to collect the sample of mud they needed if there was any other way of getting it.

'The magpies said the place we need to be is the fifth arch from this end of the bridge,' David remarked.

'Let's see if we can find something to help us,' Mary said. Then turning towards her parents continued with, 'We realize you wouldn't want us to go into the water if we can find an alternative. So let's see if we can find something as friendly as the magpies that might be able and willing to assist us.'

She had just finished speaking when the peace and quiet of the pleasant afternoon was spoiled by an awful high-pitched noise and a sort of fast flapping and buzzing sound approaching them from behind the trees. They all turned and, looking up, saw a frighteningly enormous brown dragonfly shoot over the trees and head straight down towards them. They instantly dived out of its swooping path but sadly it somehow managed to grab hold of Mary and quickly flew away with her suspended underneath its scaly body. By the time they had scrambled to their feet it was almost a third of the way across the lake and flying parallel to the side of the bridge.

David took no time at all weighing up the situation and with his right arm outstretched he pointed his forefinger at the dragonfly. It then became the recipient of a rather lethal bolt of crackling pale blue lightning. It had also just received a similar charge a split second earlier from its unwilling passenger, Mary, who had charged her own body with electricity so the dragonfly was well and truly zapped. Its wings disintegrated into dust as its writhing body exploded into hundreds of fragmented pieces covered with green mucus.

Fortunately for Mary, it had released its grip on her a couple of seconds before it exploded and she fell, narrowly missing the edge of the bridge and vanished in a big splash as she disappeared below the surface of the lake. The remaining three family members sprinted along the bridge to where she had disappeared, realizing it was the fifth arch.

In a frightened voice, Sylvia couldn't help shouting out. **'BILL! She's dropped into Offalmire's lair! I'm sure it's here. We've got to get her out, and quick!'**

David had an answer. 'Don't worry, Mum, I'll get her out.' And lying face down on the edge of the bridge he pointed both arms down towards the water, and shooting two beams down into the lake shouted, **'COME UP, SIS, COME UP THESE BEAMS.'** And before you could say 'brillfanmagical', up she came in a bouncing leap, up and on to the bridge. Her mum excitedly and emotionally enquired if she was all right and had she seen Offalmire?

Mary replied she was fine, other than being very wet and a bit muddy, and no, she hadn't seen Offalmire but she had seen the shelter that was obviously his lair.

'We weren't expecting an aerial attack though were we?' Bill remarked. 'But you two coped admirably with it.'

His dad's words prompted a humorous comment from David, who laughingly said, 'Oh, and I thought we'd done all right.'

'Just look at my trainers and legs,' Mary said, 'they're just covered in mud. I went straight to the bottom when I fell. Goodness knows why I didn't think about flying when it released me. I suppose it's because, as yet, we haven't done much of it. I've got loads of muck on me, but the best part of it is that it came out of Offalmire's lair. So without his knowledge, he's done us a really big favour. We've now got plenty of mud to add some into his poison potion, and I don't know why, but I thankfully didn't lose my cap!'

They all laughed and walked back to the start of the arched bridge, but not before scraping the mud off Mary and putting some of it into the plastic sandwich bag Sylvia brought along especially for the purpose.

Just as they reached the start of the bridge they were all taken by surprise when a large otter suddenly appeared ahead of them and strolled on to it. Having reared up to stand on its hind legs, it opened its mouth and spoke to them and they instantly recognised Merlin's voice.

Oddly, he began speaking very loudly. 'We must put our plans into action tomorrow,' he began. 'I know I said it would be tonight, but I now have it on good authority that tomorrow will be better. I have also calculated that by six o'clock tomorrow evening, King Offalmire will have become strong enough and capable enough of entering the Crystal Tower, so that is when we can stop him as he will not be aware that we can.'

Two large beady red-eyed rats that were sneaking around in the undergrowth at the end of the bridge, and which had been listening closely to every word Merlin said, giggled at being able to clearly overhear the entire plan.

Both Bill and David tried their best to interrupt Merlin, to stop him from seemingly just blurting out what they were going to do, but he simply ignored them and continued.

'Being there tomorrow evening will give you more time to prepare yourselves. You need to as there are...' he then spoke even louder, 'as there are only the four of you. You won't find it easy, if in fact you are capable of defeating Offalmire at all.'

The Knight family then realized what Merlin was doing, so they smiled and joined in the deception.

'Yes,' Bill started, 'we will do our best, Merlin. But as you say, there are only the four of us and Offalmire might have half a dozen or more helpers, and that would give us a real problem.'

Then chatting generally about the weather and what a lovely hot and sunny day it was, they slowly strolled back to their car, having first enjoyed watching the red-eyed rats scuttle off and then vanish, taking the information back to King Offalmire.

Their false plan was now set in motion and so, after bidding them all Good afternoon, Merlin also disappeared.

As they reached the car, David started to speak. 'Is that all...'

But Bill stopped him. 'I don't want us to say anything else until were safely back in the cottage and you two have created a safety barrier round it to enable us to talk. So not until then, and only then, when we are totally certain we can't be overheard by anyone or anything. Please, Son, until we get back, zip it!' And he smiled one of his knowing smiles.

Mary ran her fingers down her body, legs and trainers before getting in the car saying, 'Now be clean.' And she was.

They drove back to the cottage in total silence. Everyone wanting to say something, but trusting in Bill's sensible request to zip it...

Chapter Twenty Two

KING OFFALMIRE APPEARS

On their way back to the cottage, and just beyond the last houses on the edge of Moatcaster, the road had a number of bends in it as it twisted its way uphill. The road had been cut into the hillside so it was steeply banked on each side. Tree branches in some places reached over from both sides forming a mysterious and foreboding, dark, leafy tunnel.

Bill was just about to change to a lower gear as the hill became steeper, when without any warning and with a look of alarm and fear on his face, he was forced to bring the car to an abrupt stop. Doing so had become necessary in order to avoid running into the terrifying hulking sight which had suddenly materialized out of thin air on the road in front of them. Something resembling what might best be described as a living nightmare was now completely blocking the road. And what a horrifying sight, defying belief, it was!

A huge squat, grotesque and evil looking, hideous, slouching figure, grey green in colour with long scaly arms and short, chubby wrinkled legs stood before them. It was some sort of evil creature that looked like a cross between a huge unbelievably ugly rat and a bloated bulldog. It was wearing something that looked rather like a mud-streaked torn sail from a dinghy, which was draped from its left shoulder and wrapped round its bloated middle. It was a revoltingly ugly, horrendous sight!

Mary and her mum couldn't help screaming as everyone stared in fear and horror at its hideous, dirty, wrinkled and festering, spotty, lightly scaled face. Tufts of weird dirty brown hair stuck up from the top of its mainly bald head and on one of its many dirty chins. Both its evil looking beady eyes slowly and weirdly alternated in colour from yellow to dull red, then back again. It was a terrifying and revoltingly hideous creature that made everybody's skin creep.

Unbelievably, two candles of snot were running down from its ugly pug nose and sickeningly heading towards its now snarling mouth; a mouth displaying an evil set of stained, decayed and twisted fang-like teeth.

'That's got to be Offalmire! King Offalmire!' Sylvia exclaimed in a high pitched, terrified voice. Bill nervously had to agree, having quickly, but too late, selected reverse gear. Their car's tyres were now screaming in a cloud of blue smoke as they tried in vain to grip the road surface.

Offalmire, having taken one pounding and lurching step forward, his hideously repulsive, obnoxiously fat body shaking and wobbling like a huge jelly, had managed to grab hold of the roof rack of their car with his filthy claw-like hands, preventing their escape.

Bill, with a note of real fear in his voice, informed everyone he had locked all the doors but felt under the circumstances it was a rather futile precaution. He also suggested they loosen their seat belts, in case they needed to make a hasty retreat. They all pushed back in their seats as Offalmire's hideously revolting features came frighteningly close to the windscreen as he bent down lower trying to peer in. Bill had now given up trying to reverse. Rather unluckily for them, as the air conditioning was still on because of the heat of the day, it was drawing air in and filling the car with the revolting, sickening mixture of stenches emerging from both the front and back of Offalmire, who had belched and farted as he bent down. His filthy claw-like hands were still firmly gripping the roof rack of their car. They were now his prisoners.

Because of the stench, the Knight family's faces were all looking even more wretched, so Bill turned the air conditioning off, but left the engine running, hoping he would find a way of escaping from the stomach-churning nightmare-like event to which they were all so frighteningly and unwillingly being subjected.

From inside the car the twins tried everything they could think of to make Offalmire release his grip but nothing was working. The Master of Evil was too much for them; his immense supernatural magical power and physical strength was simply far greater and more effective than theirs.

Unwilling to give up the twins again sent a charge of electricity surging through the roof rack. The car shook violently in response.

Then, in a rough and loud voice, Offalmire bellowed out at them: 'YOU THINK YOU WERE CLEVER DON'T YOU... DROPPING INTO MY LAIR WHEN I WAS NOT THERE...AND YOU CAN FORGET YOUR PLANS FOR TOMORROW...'He belched and broke wind again. 'I HAVE NOW GAINED ENOUGH SUPERNATURAL POWER TO BE ABLE TO GET INTO THE CRYSTAL TOWER, SO ALL THE THIRTEEN TREASURES OF BRITAIN WILL SOON BE MINE, AND YOU WON'T BE ABLE TO DO A THING ABOUT IT...THIS IS WHERE YOUR JOURNEY ENDS...NOW!'

But then he made a big mistake. He released his grip on their car to raise both hands, meaning to clench them together in a huge fist type grip to smash their car with a sledgehammer blow. However, sadly for Offalmire and happily for the Knights, by doing so he unwittingly gave Bill the opportunity he had been hoping and waiting for.

Wasting no time at all, Bill whipped into reverse gear and after producing a brilliant and fast reverse spin he turned to face down the hill the way they had come. Then with tyres screaming as they shot off, they roared back down the road and into Moatcaster leaving behind a very angry King Offalmire literally frothing at the mouth and yelling that they wouldn't beat him tomorrow night.

'That has got to be the most hideous and the most grotesque and repulsive thing I have ever had the misfortune to meet and/or experience in my life,' Sylvia said. 'Given the choice, I never, ever, want to get anywhere near that obnoxious creature again.' And still shuddering as she spoke, she reminded them all that they needed to re-fasten their seat belts and went on to say, 'Evil isn't a word strong enough that accurately gets near to describing that... that hideously revolting monster! I really do hope you two, now you are the Terrestrial Twins, can and do rid the world of it tomorrow!'

'So do we, Mum, so do we!' David said, 'and I'm sure all of us feel the same way about Offalmire as you do. He is, and that was, totally nauseating and frightening, and an experience none of us would ever wish to be repeated.'

Bill reached over to touch his wife's hand in a reassuring and caring way before they all sat back in silence, each with their own private thoughts. Within a hundred yards of escaping from Offalmire, Bill had reverted to normal, steady driving. After having to divert he then turned right in Moatcaster and headed in the direction of their holiday cottage, hoping they would reach it without any more nightmare stoppages.

Having safely arrived back at their cottage and after unloading everything, David and Mary twinned, holding hands. They then created a strong safety barrier around the cottage and hoped it would give them all an opportunity to try to relax and hopefully bring their disrupted and shattered nerves and disturbed feelings back to or nearer normal.

Bill made everyone a cup of chocolate and they sat quietly on the rose patterned suite, each of them still in deep thought. Bill broke the silence, suggesting he and David should lay out all the things they had acquired for tomorrow night's event, just to make sure they had everything they would or might need. After sorting and checking, Bill said, 'We can now leave everything as it is until tomorrow. But we can't afford to miss anything out. Our lives could depend on us getting it right. We must make sure we have everything we need to win. Remember, there's no second chance! Failure is not an option!'

'But we will win, won't we, Dad?' David questioningly said. 'Offalmire can't beat us. Or can he?'

'I don't know, Son, I really don't know. But what I do know is he appears to have grown supernaturally powerful, enough to possibly break through Merlin's spell on the Crystal Tower. So I can't in all honesty answer your question. We have just got to make sure we have done, and will do, all we can to defeat him, hopefully to kill him.'

David butted in, 'But what about the poison, Dad?'

Bill replied, 'We'll mix that tomorrow afternoon...'

Sylvia then interrupted the conversation by shouting from the kitchen for them all to wash their hands as tea was ready.

'We'll sort out our final plans tomorrow, Son. The important thing is we now know that Offalmire will definitely be at Moatcaster Castle tomorrow, as he obligingly fell into our, or should I say, Merlin's trap. We also know he's going to be in that castle when **we** want him there.......we'll just have to see what tomorrow brings...'

Chapter Twenty Three

A PLAN EMERGES

Thanks to the shield the twins created around the cottage everyone had an undisturbed, though restless, night's sleep and were all surprised that none of them woke until nine o'clock.

'Do you think Merlin helped us to get a good night's sleep?' Sylvia asked Bill, as she headed for the kitchen.

'He might have, love,' Bill replied, as they started preparing breakfast together. 'He realized we all needed a proper rest for tonight's main event and he's thoughtful enough to have made sure we all got one.'

Bill then went to knock on the twins' doors to make sure they got up. 'Come on, you two, breakfast is almost ready.'

After showering and having enjoyed and thanked their mum for an excellent breakfast, the twins washed and dried, then put away the breakfast pots. Then they all sat round the table to hold a very important 'council of war'. A brain-storming session, discussing as to what their strategies and tactics might be and deciding which of the various bits and pieces they had acquired would be going with them and how all the items would possibly to be used.

'The castle closes at six o'clock,' Bill said. 'I expect it takes up to about seven or eight o'clock to clean up after everyone has left, so I suggest we park near the castle at around seven-thirty. We will need to look round for a while, so if you two can first transport us to the top of the King's Tower or near it, a little before eight o'clock that should be fine. We will then be able to have a good look round from up there. Members of the public will not be able to see us anyway, as we will be in our own supernatural parallel time slot.'

'Also, since we have no idea when or how Offalmire and his cronies will arrive in the castle grounds, being on top of the King's Tower or high up somewhere will give us a practical and strategic position from which to reconnoiter.'

Sylvia joined in saying, 'From what Merlin has told us, we know Offalmire will make his move **tonight,** so we just have to make sure we are really ready for him and whoever else he brings. So let's have a look at what we've got.'

Picking up the items one at a time from the table, and discussing each of them and their uses, they sensibly and carefully reviewed each piece of their arsenal. The two backpacks they brought on holiday were to be worn by Bill and Sylvia. The two new ones were for the twins. Bill said they were to be worn on their chests, not on their backs, as doing so would make them more readily accessible, enabling them to retrieve from them what they might require more easily and quickly.

The belts they were unable to buy were replaced by their bum bags which they always wore anyway. Wearing them would enable all the family members to carry knives or anything else they chose to take.

'But what are the balloons for?' Mary asked.

David chimed in, 'And the screw-top bottles? What are they for, Dad?'

Sylvia was the first to answer, 'The balloons will be partially filled with milk to be used as bombs.'

'That's a great idea, Mum,' David said, 'that stuff really doesn't suit them, does it? They really don't like milk.'

'And the bottles,' Bill said, 'are to be filled with water.' He then grinned. 'I mentioned it before and I know it's a bit odd, but everything that makes up your bodies or is or has been part of you, will be totally lethal to all evil entities from the Dark Side, as is milk. So the water we have been talking about and are taking in the bottles you two bought, is to be provided by you two.'

'You're right there, it is a bit odd. In fact, it's more than a bit odd. I reckon it's a bit gross, Dad, especially coming from you.' And David pretended to screw up his face.

Mary couldn't help butting in and raised a smile saying, 'But it's not going to be coming from Dad, is it? It's going to be coming from us!' Then turning to her mother she asked, 'But is Dad really serious, Mum?'

'Yes, love, he most certainly is. Merlin knew how important it is, that's why he included it in the list of ingredients for the poison potion, so we will need some later for that as well. And do you remember what happened to those two little goblins your Dad sucked up from behind the fridge that ended up in the loo?'

'And have you forgotten the swords in the gent's loo yesterday,' David enjoyed saying.

'We really do need every bit of useful ammunition we can put together for tonight,' Bill said, 'so let's get serious,' his voice now taking on a firmer tone. 'We're not talking about gallons, and it does make an awful lot of sense. As you both are able to provide us with something we know can really help, you will gladly. And there's no reason why you can't start now. I have put some bottles in the bathroom. Just make sure you each leave your bottles on different sides of the room for when we're mixing the potion. It's really no different than having to take a specimen to the nurse or doctor, so let's get serious and act a little more grown-up and stop behaving as though you were little children.'

'I hope you weren't expecting me to say something to that, Dad,' David said, having decided to go to the bathroom, 'Coz if you were...Hang on a minute though, shouldn't it be ladies first?'

'Stop him, Mum!' Mary said appealing to her mother, 'he's just embarrassing me.'

'Don't take things so seriously, love,' Sylvia replied, 'your brother's only making light of what is a pretty heavy situation we all find ourselves in.'

'Don't worry, Sis,' David said heading for the bathroom, 'I'll start and **go** first,' then picking up speed, he jokingly said as he dashed in, '**I'll just whiz in here now**,' and closed the door.

'David!' his mum remarked, 'But then, I suppose I should be glad he's not lost his sense of humour.'

'But...but...do I, do I really have to...well, you know what, Mum?'

'Yes you do, my little princess,' her mum replied, 'but I'll have a word with you in the bathroom, when David comes out.' Mary smiled and nodded her appreciation.

Making adjustments to straps, part filling balloons with milk and putting together and preparing everything they might need took up a fair chunk of the morning.

The twins then said they wanted to go into David's bedroom as they had a couple of things to discuss and try. So their mum made glasses of orange which she took into them just as David had started to say, 'If we hold hands and try twinning, we might be able to reach him.'

'I think I'll leave you two alone for a while,' Sylvia said, 'perhaps you need to practise some twinning on your own.' And she left the twins to their own devices.

'Right,' David said, 'let's hold hands and concentrate really hard, we might be able to reach them with our thought waves by telepathy. It works for us.'

Bill had a big grin on his face as Sylvia returned to the lounge. 'You're a very devious woman you are, Missus Knight.'

'Who, sir, me, sir, surely not?' she joked with her husband.

'Yes, you,' he said, still broadly grinning, 'do you think the twins have any idea why you keep giving them orange?'

'I think it might dawn on one if not both of them a little later, if it hasn't already. But I don't think David will say anything. Knowing how his mind works, or at least I used to, he'll just think it's all a bit different and amusing.'

Back in David's bedroom, the twins sensed they were about to be successful with their first attempt at telepathy twinning. 'Hello, Red, can you hear us? Are you receiving us? We would very much like to talk with you if we can.'

Fortunately the twins didn't have long to wait, for in the form of a slightly faded picture, Red's image appeared on the bedroom wall, which delighted them both.

'Hello, you two. What a very nice surprise, it's so good to be able see and speak with you, especially like this. In what way might I be of assistance to you?'

Both twins were delighted they had been successful in their first attempt at twinning telepathy when a third party was involved, particularly as they had been able to communicate with and have a long chat with Red.

'We could talk to Sir Gawain as well,' Mary said.

'I spoke to him when we were at Bowtown Hall,' David added, 'so we don't need to call him again until tonight.'

'How about some fish and chips for lunch?' Sylvia shouted from the kitchen. 'It will save me having to cook.'

'Sounds great!' David and Mary said emerging from the bedroom, their faces beaming.

Turning to David, Bill said, 'We'll get them, Son. Mary, can help your mum?'

'We'll leave the barrier round the cottage, Mum,' David said, 'I'll put one round the car as well. They will help us all relax a bit.' Everyone agreed, and off the guys went to the chippy.

They had just entered the lane on the way back when David asked his dad to stop for a second or two. Having got out, he went over to have a quick word with a black and white cow which they had discovered was called Mabel. It was a small herd so the farmer had given names to all his cattle. Mabel was the cow Bill had surprisingly milked and which had splattered the goblin in the barrow when they were fighting the unwelcome guests in the garden.

After returning to the car and re-fitting his seat belt, David informed his dad that Mabel would be happy to supply more milk when they needed it. 'I thought your mum had bought enough milk, Son, but it's good that we can have some more if and when we want some.'

Everyone enjoyed eating the fish and chips lunch, and David slightly annoyed everyone by again joking about the peas. As the suite in the lounge had become their favourite place to relax, they all sat for a while looking at the newspapers, magazines and comics which Bill and David had brought back from town.

The bottles in the bathroom containing the contents for the bombs steadily increased in number as the day moved on and Sylvia continued to supply the twins with orange drinks. Bill just looked on with a knowing smile on his face. A smile that bravely hid the torment his emotions were going through. The torment of not knowing what the confrontation, this battle his family was destined to have with the evil King Offalmire, might bring in a few hours' time...

Chapter Twenty Four

MIXING THE POISON POTION

'All right everybody! It's now time to mix the poison potion,' Sylvia announced in a very positive voice. 'I think we'll do it in the kitchen. We can put the waterproof picnic blanket on the table and cover it with newspapers. That way we won't have any problems if there are any splashes.'

After making the bucket containing the special ingredients re-appear, David carefully placed it next to the table on a chair.

'We'll check everything off the list as we put them in the pan,' Sylvia said, 'we don't want to miss anything out. This is too important a mixture to get wrong.'

Mary handed her mum the container in which they had kept Merlin's parchment safely hidden. Having carefully removed it, Sylvia began to check off the items that were so important, before placing them into the sizeable two-handled pan specially bought by her in Moatcaster in which to mix the poison potion.

'Hair of badger,' Sylvia said, with a strange tone in her voice as she took the clump of hair from David and placed it in the pan. She then continued, 'Mistletoe of oak marinated in leek broth.'

'How on earth are we going to do that, Mum?' asked a worried David.

'Easy, Son, calm down. Pass me those leeks we bought in Moatcaster, Mary. They're in the fridge. We'll just chop them up with the leaves of mistletoe and pop them straight into the pan. They will form a broth with everything else as they all steadily boil together.'

Mary then chopped both ingredients and carefully popped them in the pan.

'Venom of vipers next,' Sylvia said.

'It's in this carton, David,' his dad said, 'and be careful.' And he was. He didn't want any on himself, but more importantly he didn't want to spill any. And he didn't. He then washed the knife he had used to scrape the last drop out of the container under running water from the tap in the sink.

'Now, droppings of a bat please, Mary.'

Bill passed her the crisp bag into which they had been deposited saying, 'That was a night none of us will ever forget, especially as you two made such a big splash.' But as they were all concentrating on what they were doing, no one smiled.

'Now be careful with this one,' Sylvia mused having asked for droppings of a red dragon. The twins took a step back as their dad carefully emptied a couple of tennis ball sized pieces into the pan from the carrier bag in which it had been kept.

'That stuff reeks almost like Offalmire did,' David said, holding his nose.

But his mum, totally ignoring him, went on to say, 'and the next one is…a drop of two virgins' blood. And no more supposedly humorous comments from you, David either. All right?'

'Yes, Mum! But how are we going to do it?'

'I can do what nurses do. I can prick your ear or your finger and squeeze a drop out.' A comment which made both twins cringe.

'Or,' Bill said, grinning as he picked up a knife from the table, 'I could cut you with this.'

'I think we'll settle for a pricked finger if you don't mind, Dad, thanks,' David joked, 'but it was good of you to offer!' Sylvia had already sterilized a needle from her emergency sewing kit with some of Bill's aftershave, but did it again before and between squeezing a couple of drops of blood onto a small tissue from each twin before dropping it into the pan.

'A drop of good stuff that,' David joked sucking his thumb. His mum again totally ignored him as she asked for the next item.

'Now the blood sap from the Bowtown Hall yew trees,' and Bill scraped it from its carton onto another small piece of tissue then dropped it into the pan.

'We must be particularly careful with this one,' Sylvia said, as David passed the bottle of water they had collected from St. Morn's Well, and she slowly poured it all into the pan.

'And the last of the collected ingredients is the mud from King Offalmire's lair,' she then went on to say, 'fortunately it only smells like the bottom of the lake and nothing like his putrid odour we experienced yesterday. I thought for a minute that I was going to be sick. He's totally obnoxious.'

'I think we all feel the same, love,' Bill said, 'I can't think of anything more revolting or repugnantly evil than him.'

'Well, that's almost everything in the pot and we have the wooden love spoon to stir it. What we need now, I think, is about two pints of tap water. Oh and yes, I'm also going to put in a drop of milk. We know it doesn't do them a lot of good either. All that's missing now…is some water from you two.'

'And there's no need to throw a fit about it either,' Bill said, having noticed their facial expressions and body language following their mother's request. 'I'll simply bring in a couple of bottles from the bathroom. You did put them at different sides of the room as we asked, didn't you?' Both twins turned and looked at each other for a couple of seconds before together saying with a smile, 'Of course, Dad, you don't think we would let you down, do you?' Bill shrugged his shoulders and went into the bathroom for the bottles.

Having got all the ingredients in the cooking pot, Sylvia informed them that the potion needed to gently boil on a low cooker number for about half an hour. It would then need to simmer for a further half hour with everyone taking a turn at stirring it using the love spoon.

'Once it is almost done,' Sylvia instructed, ' your dad will put the pan in the middle of the table for you two to do your nude chanting dance round it.'

Mary just about erupted. **No! No! No! No way, Mum!** There is no way I am going to dance naked with David.'

'And I don't want to dance naked with **her** either,' was David's retorting reply.

'Now calm down you two, calm down!' Sylvia said, 'there's no need to get upset at all. You both **will** dance naked as instructed on Merlin's parchment, but you will simply do it separately, totally privately on your own. That way there won't be a problem, but both of you will still have fully completed the important instructions.'

'But do I really need to take **all** my clothes off?' Mary nervously asked.

'To be brutally honest, love,' Bill said, 'if we don't get what we are doing right, not only can we say goodbye to our chance of killing King Offalmire but we may also lose our own lives! So I hope that answers your question…Do you really want to be the reason for us failing our mission, the special mythological reason why we are all here, to complete your planned destiny?'

'Steady, love,' Sylvia said, 'did you really need to be that hard on her, she's really upset now.'

'I'm sorry you're upset, love,' Bill said as he put his arm lovingly round his daughter's shoulders, 'but you have to realize that whatever it is we have to do, **we have to do it!** Our own personal feelings and emotions have to be put to one side until it's all over. You stir the pan for a minute or two. It will help you get your thoughts into perspective.'

Sylvia opened the kitchen window and door at this point as the air was becoming soured to say the least.

Everyone continued taking their turn at stirring with the love spoon, so it wasn't long before the potion was fully stewed and ready. Bill then carefully removed the pan from the cooker and placed it on to the newspaper in the centre of the kitchen table. All that remained to complete the preparation of the supernatural poison potion was for the twins to each do their naked chanting dance.

David, being the perfect gentleman as ever, suggested that Mary be first. Their mum then thoughtfully ushered her daughter into her bedroom to give her a brief loving mother-to-daughter prep talk.

Mary shortly emerged from her room into the lounge, barefoot and wearing her dressing robe. 'You're not cheating under there?' David jokingly asked as she quickly walked through.

'No I'm not!' she snapped back, loosening her belt as she dashed into the kitchen and closed the door.

Sylvia had left Bill's copy of the poison chant on the table and the three of them listened to Mary recite and chant Merlin's verse as she three times circled the table.

To fight and defeat King Offalmire's power
Mix the potion before second sixth hour
In Terrestrial Twins' water must bubble this spell
Speak naught to no one lest they leave and tell
The Yew Tree Arrow must find Offalmire's eye
With the Sacred God's Light, evil Offalmire will die.

'That was embarrassing,' Mary said as she came out of the kitchen, meeting and passing David in the centre of the lounge. He was now barefoot and wearing his robe, and on his way through for his stint in the kitchen.

He had just passed his sister when, as he had done, she asked, 'Are **you** cheating?' at the same time grabbing the collar of his robe. David then gave out an embarrassed yell, for as he started to dash for the kitchen his robe came off in Mary's hand.

The three of them then witnessed the sight of his naked back and backside as he shot into the kitchen and slammed the door behind him. That left Mary to accompany their parents in fits of uncontrollable laughter as she stood in the centre of the lounge holding David's robe in her hand. The three of them then listened as best they could between bouts of laughter to David loudly reciting three verses of the chant.

This was followed by almost a minute of total silence as they waited for David to emerge. Mary joined her parents seated on the couch and, like them, had her eyes firmly fixed on the door to the kitchen, all of them had what looked like permanent silly grins of anticipation on their faces.

The kitchen door then very slowly opened just a little way, giving a further boost to the tense and excited anticipation the three of them were experiencing as they sat waiting for David to re-appear. David then totally amazed the three of them when he opened the door fully and slowly walked out…

To say it looked like they were having laughter fits, is an understatement. For David, as only he could, as bold as brass, slowly strolled across the room wearing nothing but a big smile on his face and his mother's little kitchen apron. What an amusing sight he made. Just over halfway across the lounge, and to even more fits of laughter, he made a dash for his room, his hands attempting to cover his bottom as he almost leapt into his bedroom. The three family members were still tittering when he came out wearing a pair of black shorts and with a big beaming smile on his face he sat down.

'I think that did all of us the world of good,' Bill said. 'That was a really good family tonic. Thank you, Son, we needed that.'

But that was not all…There was more to come… What happened next was what might have been described as almost a life-changing total shock for David and his parents. In fact they were all truly amazed at what Mary did, which for her was so much out of character. She, seemingly not wishing to be outdone by her brother, took everyone totally by surprise by doing something which had them laughing even more.

After standing up and moving three paces towards her bedroom, and having reached the point when everyone would only be able to see her back, Mary loosened her belt and shocked everyone by completely slipping out of her robe and holding it draped over her right shoulder. Then, strolling like a model on a catwalk, she threw her head back and progressed slowly to her room, dragging her dressing robe behind her. She then turned her head to smile and nod her appreciation at the spontaneous applause from the three seated, shocked and very surprised family members as she slinked into her bedroom and closed the door.

'Well I never!' pronounced her mother, still a little shocked. 'I do believe my little princess has just demonstrated she isn't so little anymore. From now on she'll be our Castershire Princess, Bill, the name my parents used to call me.' The two male members of the family, still looking a bit shell-shocked, smiled and nodded their heads in agreement.

Bill, with a laugh in his voice, had the last word. 'I think they were both proud to show us that neither of them was cheating.'

After a light tea, as no one was feeling particularly hungry, they finished making the poison potion which Sylvia had allowed to simmer down to thicken. Having first allowed the contents of the pan to cool, it was carefully poured into a screw-top jar from which Sylvia had removed the jam. It was then placed into their black carry-all with the other items they might possibly need later, the twins having first made sure that all items were magically protected.

Addressing David, his father asked, 'You did talk to Sir Gawain and tell him about the importance of the bow and arrow, didn't you, Son?'

'Yes, Dad, he's totally tuned in to what we want him to do and will arrive the moment we call him or if he's needed.'

'Good,' Bill replied. 'The bow and arrow are so crucially important to the success of our mission and to what we will be attempting to accomplish in just a few hours time, I would hate anything to go wrong.'

Sylvia joined in saying, 'Merlin said he would be near at hand if there were any major problems, and we know the Gods of the Terrestrial Light are aware we need their Supernatural Special Light to help finish off Offalmire, so I do think everything is ready, love.'

She then continued with, 'We've all got milk bombs in balloons, spray cream in aerosol cans and the twins' water in bottles, and I've made sure there are sufficient quantities in the rucksacks we'll each be wearing on our chests, plus we'll all be wearing our bum bags for knives and things. Your father even managed to buy a large toy water cannon when we went to the supermarket.'

'What have you filled it with, Dad?' David jumped in quickly and asked with a big grin on his face.

'Sorry to disappoint you, Son, it's filled with milk.'

'It's a coincidence though,' David said, 'I found a water pistol in the back of the cupboard, but that's got the real thing in. It's going in my bum bag belt with a couple of kitchen knives.'

'I will have a couple of knives in my belt too,' Mary said, 'and I know Mum will be doing the same.'

'And I've put some extra knives and some forks in my belt and bag and in the carry-all as an extra precaution,' Bill said.

'Why forks, Dad?' Mary asked.

'I will be able to throw them accurately and stand an even better chance of bursting balloons with them if I need to,' Bill replied. 'But what I think we should all do now is to sit quietly and try to relax a little. You can read a book or a magazine, or if you like we can have a game of dominoes. We've brought them with us as we always do when we go on holiday.'

'What a brillfanmagical idea, Dad,' David said. 'They're all black and white like our logo and our magical colours. Perhaps they'll be a good omen and will bring us good luck! And, as we haven't seen or heard anything from the aliens, Mary and I feel we now won't. If they had intended to do anything else, it would have already happened. Or that's what we think...'

Chapter Twenty Five

JUST A LITTLE SURPRISE

It had been another hot day and the evening was still pleasantly warm. After the twins had spoken a quick word or two with the magpies perched on the garden fence, they left the cottage a little before six o'clock, the twins having first created a protective shield on their car to ensure they would all arrive alive at Moatcaster Castle.

Whatever it was that was shortly to happen, they hoped it was going to be the successful climax to the reason David and Mary had become the Terrestrial Twins and the reason they were in Castershire; their destiny.

All their gear had been twice checked to ensure nothing was missing, particularly the screw-topped jam jar containing the crucially important magical potion. They had all agreed from now on, rather than call it the poison jar, they would refer to it as the 'P' jar, a name thought up by the twins.

They all looked very smart in their favourite outfits, their black 'Bill Knight's Seven Magpies Martial Arts Studio' strip; all of them having opted to wear shorts rather than tracksuit bottoms with it being so warm. With their caps topping their impressive outfits, they looked a really formidable team.

Bill, helped by David, had even washed their car which also looked particularly smart and ready for action, as it always did, proudly displaying their Seven Magpies logo on both front doors. They all wanted to look as well as to feel good on this a very different and especially important evening. Hopefully, it would be their final confrontation with the evil and repulsive King Offalmire.

Each member of the Knight family now experienced a mixture of private thoughts and feelings, particularly of nervousness and apprehension, as they neared Moatcaster Castle — and it was understandable. None of them had any idea as to what the next couple of hours or so might bring. They were all understandably feeling rather tense as they were aware that the outcome of the confrontation in the castle which was shortly to take place was so fundamentally important, yet unknown.

The twins, as they knew their parents would also be, were fully aware of their responsibilities but understandably anxious as to what might actually happen in their encounter with King Offalmire, even though they were now the Terrestrial Twins. As they had only recently acquired supernatural abilities, they were obviously still unaware as to what they were capable of, their powers being so new to them. They had no idea as to the range, strengths or limits of whatever it was they had been blessed with by the Gods of the Terrestrial Light. Were they really capable of winning such an important fight against such a gross, evil and formidable supernatural opponent as King Offalmire?

They were even more concerned about their parents' safety than their own, and their parents were naturally worried about them. In fact, the whole family just wished it was all over so they could get back to normality and to enjoying the rest of their Castershire holiday.

Bill was fortunately able to park close to the castle near the bridge and said as he reversed in, 'It will soon be seven o'clock. We'll wait here until about ten minutes past, then, as we planned, we'll go to the rear of the castle below the chute from the King's Banqueting Hall where Red lives so that you two can somehow get us into the castle.' Facing the twins he went on to say, 'You both said you had a little surprise about the way you would be getting us in, kids, and I have to confess your mother and I are not only curious about that, we're even a little apprehensive.'

'No need to worry, Dad!' David replied. 'Trust me! I promise it will only be a little surprise.'

Having arrived at the back of Moatcaster Castle below the King's Banqueting Hall, David moved close to thrust his face up to the bars and peering up the chute shouted, 'Are you okay Red, and are you ready?'

'Yes I am, and yes I am,' came back the amusing reply.

'What's he ready for?' Sylvia asked.

'Anything, Mum, anything!' was David's smiling reply. At that moment the seven friendly and magical magpies surprised Bill and Sylvia when they materialized on the path close to where they were standing. But that wasn't all! The twins' parents were even more amazed to hear their daughter say, 'Good, your transport has arrived!'

Then the twins managed to surprise them one more time when together, and while seemingly drawing an invisible circle round them with their outstretched free hands, their other hands being firmly gripped in a twinning stance, said, 'For us all to fly up onto the wall, our twinning now must make us small.' And their extraordinary magical powers instantly worked.

To the total amazement of their parents, all four of them steadily shrunk to about the size of a tennis ball. Mary jokingly saying, 'David told you it would only be a **little surprise!**'

She was then interrupted by the lead magpie saying, as he lowered his left wing, 'Climb on board, climb up on to my back. We'll have you safely up there in no time at all.' The three other magpies then also lowered their wings.

To say their parents were astounded and completely gob-smacked is an understatement!

It was a remarkable sight to see as the Knight family climbed up the wings and mounted their feathered and magical taxi transports and then sat straddle legged across their individual magpie's neck. Then up into the air they went, steadily climbing in a rising flight path, flying in single file above the footpath and parallel to the castle wall and the river. It was as they were turning to the right, following the shape of the castle wall that they flew into trouble. A huge hawk appeared and shot across the front of the lead magpie attempting to dislodge David who was riding on it, and who was now gripping its neck as tightly as he could.

'Damn that Offalmire moron and all his helpers,' the lead magpie said. Then shouted, '**HOLD ON REALLY TIGHT EVERYBODY WHILE THE FOUR OF US MAKE A DEFENSIVE MANOEUVRE. THE OTHER THREE, OUR BACK-UP TEAM WILL DEAL WITH THE HAWK!**'

It then shot up in the air and back around in a very tight complete 'loop the loop' circular manoeuvre, the other three magpies doing exactly the same as they closely followed their leader.

What a sight it was, as the four taxi magpies zoomed at an alarming speed out of their aerial display and to safety. All the Knight family could do was to hang on to the necks of their taxi magpies like limpets. They simply left the hawk behind looking rather puzzled as it hovered, wondering what had happened and what to do next.

The three back-up magpies didn't waste any time. Using their supernatural strength they easily saw off the unwary hawk. Having together dropped on to it like a stone, they quickly and efficiently forced it down to the river. Then tightly gripping hold of it, they submerged taking it with them. The three magpies then magically transformed into otters as they dragged the helpless hawk beneath the surface of the river.

The remaining relatively short flight to the top of the castle's ramparts was trouble free and the four clever magical magpies carefully set the Knight family down on to the roof of the Queen's Tower, where the four family members instantly returned to their normal sizes. After saying and squawking their goodbyes, the friendly magpies disappeared.

'I love this magical stuff, love,' Sylvia said addressing her husband.

Bill replied with a big smile on his face, 'I think I could get to like it too, Sylv'.'

Having glanced around the area Sylvia continued, 'It all looks quiet to me.'

'The trouble is, that is when it's most dangerous,' Bill said, 'when you can't see anybody or anything. This is the time we need to be very, very careful. But as everywhere does appear to be clear, let's change our position and move to a different viewing post. Please fly us over to the Prince's Tower kids, we should see more from there.'

After the twins had transported all of them across, David said, 'You were right, Dad, we've got a much better overall view of most of the castle from here, but I have to tell you, I am now sensing something evil, very evil.'

'Me too,' Mary said, 'and whatever or whoever it is, it's growing bigger and stronger. I am also getting a feeling of foreboding, as though something evil is about to happen.'

She was right about that, for having spoken her last word a figure appeared out of thin air on the wall between the Cell's Tower and the King's Tower. Taking the Knight family completely by surprise, they saw that the figure was wearing the uniform of a Roundhead soldier.

'It's a ruddy goblin dressed as a Roundhead,' David blurted out, 'but why, why a Roundhead?'

Bill, ignoring his son's understandable outburst, came up with an answer. 'Oliver Cromwell and his Roundhead soldiers once attacked this castle. It looks as though King Offalmire has somehow supernaturally managed to merge his goblin warriors with what were Roundhead soldiers and is using them to fight for him. Let's hope there aren't going to be many of them, or we could be in real trouble.'

Unfortunately, they became even more disappointed to see three more Roundheads appear as he spoke, and sadly that wasn't the end of it. Four more soldiers materialized out of thin air to form an evil and threatening line across the wall in front of the King's Tower.

'Hell, that's eight,' spluttered David, 'it looks like we are going to need reinforcements.'

'No real problem there, David. There are only a few of them,' a voice speaking from behind them said, making them all jump. It was Sir Gawain their friendly knight who had materialized and who now looked magnificent in his suit of black and white light armour. He had sensed the tension and understandably some growing fear in the family and knew it was time he made an appearance.

'Don't do that,' remarked Mary, addressing Sir Gawain, 'you just about made all of us jump out of our skins. But we are all very pleased to see you. 'And she gave him a hug, which brought a big smile to his face.

'I'm just glad I went to the toilet before I came out,' David joked.

'I thought you might need me,' Sir Gawain said. 'I sensed you were all feeling tense, so here I am at your service,' and he bowed. 'I have the yew tree bow and arrow with me. Should I poison the arrow tip now or later?'

'Now is a good time,' Bill replied, 'as we don't know when it will be needed.' Taking the 'P' jar from the carryall as he spoke he removed the lid as he turned towards Sir Gawain.

'That's an excellent idea, a turning top,' Sir Gawain innocently remarked, which amused everyone but they politely didn't let it show. 'I really like that idea. Do you think other people might want one of those?'

'Yes, it is a good idea, Sir Gawain,' Sylvia said in an effort to politely close the conversation, 'and they are very popular. Many people have them and find them very useful. They are known as screw-top jars.'

The resplendent looking knight had carefully selected an arrow fitted with black and white flight feathers from the quiver suspended from his belt while Sylvia was speaking and handing it to Bill said, 'This is the special yew tree arrow. I made the flights from feathers kindly given to me by two magpies. We thought their magic would also help.'

As Bill removed the arrow's tip from the jar after dipping it in the 'P' potion, Sir Gawain went on to say, 'If you look closely, you will see I created some small holes in the arrow head which will help to carry more poison.' He then demonstrated how powerful and how tightly strung the special yew tree bow was, and finished by proudly saying, 'They are both now ready to carry out their crucially important task, ridding the world of that evil monstrosity King Offalmire.'

As everyone thanked him for doing such a terrific job, an unbelievably obnoxious foul smell drifted up on a breeze from the direction of the King's Tower, sickeningly assaulting their nostrils. Simultaneously their faces screwed-up and, as though they had rehearsed it, everyone uttered one word: 'Offalmire!'

He had invisibly transported himself to appear on the far side of the King's Tower near to its ground level entrance, where he had been joined by five more Roundhead goblins. What a frightening, formidable and ominous sight they made, especially the grotesque image of King Offalmire.

'Just look at that lot,' David said very nervously, as he mentally counted the total of the opposition, 'are we going to be able to cope with that many?'

Calmly, Sir Gawain answered him, 'I am more than confident that we can and will, David. After all, there are only thirteen of them. Do you really think they are capable of defeating **us**?' And he paused. 'We are five Knights, and two of our squad are the Terrestrial Twins. Also, as I am one of the most successful knights to ever take up battle arms in Castershire, I am most confident we can do battle with and defeat these unspeakably evil entities and win.'

'Sir Gawain is right, Son,' Bill said, pride in his voice. 'We're here to do a job and I feel sure the job we are about to do will be a first rate one, a successful one. We have yours and Mary's newly acquired strengths and abilities plus Sir Gawain's experience and fighting capability. So, collectively with your mum and I backing you up with our skills, we should be more than enough to help the pair of you successfully complete the task with which you have been charged, for as I said earlier, failure is not an option!'

'I wish I had thought of that phrase,' Sir Gawain said with a big smile on his face as he turned to address Sylvia. 'Have no fear, my lady,' he charmingly said, 'I feel confident that the twins can do much to ensure the safety of us all but have yet to learn the range of their abilities. However, I wish to ensure you I consider it an honour and my respectful and personal duty to ensure no harm befalls you, the lady of the household. And let us not forget...I have the special magical killing bow and arrow.'

'Come and hold my hands, Sis,' David said, a strong but caring tone in his voice. 'Grip them both really tightly and let's show Offalmire and his warriors what twinning and our Terrestrial Twins' strengths and powers are all about. I feel you and I are now ready for anything, Sis.'

Having reached for and grasped each other's hands, they both tightened their grip and crossed their arms in the full twinning exercise. That done, the twins looked across in the direction of Offalmire and both began to mumble something. They then released their twinning hold to enable them to point the forefingers of their right hands in the direction of his grotesque shape. What happened next took the twins' parents and even Sir Gawain totally by surprise as the twins together loudly shouted...**'OFFALMIRE SO UGLY, SO FOUL AND SO TALL, YOUR EVIL POWER IS WEAKENED AS WE NOW SHRINK YOU SMALL!'**

At the same time, bolts of thin shimmering blue light flashed from each of their pointing forefingers and shot across the space between them and twined round and round his grotesque body. King Offalmire was now totally enclosed in a pale blue and white shimmering light which lasted for about seven seconds. The light then faded and Offalmire shook himself and gave out three huge bellowing roars of anger. This terrified the thirteen goblin Roundheads so much it brought most of them quivering and cowering to their knees.

Many of them were moaning in fear of what the bellowing and screaming Offalmire might do to them now he was so angry as he had already hurt some of them on previous occasions.

At the same time the Knights' squad, and with total delight, witnessed the sight of Offalmire's grotesque evil body firstly begin to uncontrollably tremble then convulsively shake. As the volume of shaking began to reduce, so unbelievably did the bulk of Offalmire. He was getting smaller and smaller as he amazingly, magically continued to shrink before their eyes.

Then in a tormented, almost hysterical rage, after he'd unbelievably and helplessly shrunk to less than half of his original size, and whilst stamping his feet and whirling about in anger, King Offalmire bellowed-out an order. 'THEY ARE ON THE PRINCE'S TOWER...THREE OF YOU POOR EXCUSES FOR WARRIORS, GO AND KILL THEM! KILL THEM ALL! KILL THEM NOW!'

Obeying Offalmire's raging commands, three of the nearest Roundheads, swords drawn, hurtled themselves up and on to the ramparts at the top of the wall. They looked like trouble.

Sir Gawain shouting, 'KNIGHTS FOREVER!' and with his sword drawn, sprang to meet them. In what was no more than a one-sided skirmish, he quickly disposed of the first Roundhead with brilliant swordplay and then took on the second, who proved to be a slightly better swordsman.

Whilst Sir Gawain was engaged with him, the third goblin leaped over his head and began to menacingly approach the Knight family group, a sword in one hand, a knife in the other.

'Here goes,' David said as he took one of the balloon milk bombs out of the rucksack on his chest. The goblin then unwittingly did David a big favour for as the milk bomb came hurtling through the air at him he made the absolutely fatal mistake of sticking his sword in it, and was more than surprised to receiving a good dousing of milk for his effort.

The expression of shocked surprise quickly disappeared from his face as the milk which had sprayed all over him had the usual effect. Shrieking in agony, his body uncontrollably jerking and writhing, he toppled off the ramparts to become nothing more than a heaving pile of snotty, muddy uniform.

The second goblin still fighting with Sir Gawain then went the same way as the first, but minus its head, as Sir Gawain severed it from its shoulders with a really powerful swirling blow. Sir Gawain turned back to face Sylvia, a smile on his face as he said, 'Three down, only ten to go... They really don't like milk though, do they?'

As all eyes had been looking in the direction of the action on the ramparts, no one had noticed the column of dark green smoke which Offalmire had dispatched and beamed to where the Knight family was standing. Like an obnoxiously smelling smoke screen, it took them all by surprise as it totally engulfed the whole of the top of the tower. They couldn't see a thing.

Coughing and spluttering they stumbled out on to the ramparts. Then Bill, with understandable panic in his voice said, 'Where is she? ......**Where's Mary?**'

The awful smoke cleared and he dashed to where they had all been standing less than a minute earlier. But there was no sign of Mary. His lovely daughter was not there... She had gone. Offalmire had taken her.

Naturally, being the loving father he was, Bill just about erupted. 'That filthy and wretched evil...' he started to swear, then stopped and apologized to his wife for his language. But under the circumstances, Sylvia really hadn't expected him to apologize. Their daughter had been kidnapped!

'That evil obnoxious swine has taken our daughter, your sister, David. We've got to get her back. We've just got to get her back. What if he's harmed her? What if...?' He stopped...then continued... 'David, Sir Gawain, we've got to find her and get her back or that evil creature will probably hurt her, possibly might even kill her...'

'Calm down, love,' Sylvia said as she caught hold of Bill's arm, 'calm down or you'll have a heart attack. I'm upset too, but as you always say we have to keep our heads or that evil monster is going to win, so please, Bill, let's just think.'

David joined in at this point with some very grown-up words, 'Mum's right, Dad. We can all see and understand why you are so upset. You're blaming yourself for not being able to protect your daughter but there was nothing, absolutely nothing you, me, Sir Gawain or Mum could have done to prevent what happened. We are all struggling against and fighting some of the most powerful magic in the world, so sometimes it just might be able to get the better of us. But it's only temporary and we'll be back on top before you know it. I have no doubt we'll soon have Sis back with us. We have to continue trusting ourselves and our abilities. We are a formidable team and we are going to do our damnedest to make sure it is us who win.'

'Well said, young Knight, I could not have explained it better myself,' Sir Gawain said, 'so what is it that you now choose to do, young sir? I am ready for anything. You lead and I will gladly assist you...'

Chapter Twenty Six

THE FINAL BATTLE

'Okay,' David said after managing to subdue his father and reassure his mum that he was confident that everything would soon be all right. 'This is the plan. You, Dad will stay here to look after Mum.' His mum smiled, understanding what her son was doing. 'Sir Gawain will come with me. We will be able to see more from the top of the King's Tower, so that's where we need to go.' He then grabbed Sir Gawain's hand and they quickly flew over to the roof of the King's Tower.

'We can now look straight down and get a better picture of what is happening,' David said, a strong tone in his voice.

'I have to say, David, that was a stroke of genius shrinking the size of Offalmire as you did,' Sir Gawain said, 'that must have also helped in reducing his magical powers.'

'That was the general idea,' David replied, 'let's hope it was worth it and it worked.'

The foul stench of Offalmire drifted up and reminded them he wasn't very far away, not that they needed reminding, and David carefully peered over the edge. 'Thank goodness, Mary appears to be all right. Offalmire is holding her close to him, so sadly she's trapped against the side of his stinking body by his dirty, smelly hand and arm, and that can't really be good. But we have to be more than glad that she's still alive.'

'Because he's holding her so close to him, even though his supernatural powers are reduced, they're still strong enough to prevent her from being able to use hers. Can you transport yourself down, Sir Gawain, and keep them occupied? I'll go and get my parents and tell them Mary appears to be okay. This is a great position from which to be able to bombard them.'

'It will be my pleasure, David, and I thank you again for the opportunity to enjoy some real fun,' and down he went to enjoy another skirmish with the goblin Roundheads.

No sooner had David left to collect his parents than he was back with them on the top of the King's Tower. Then speaking to them as they became more settled, he said, 'Mary's all right! She's alive and doesn't appear injured, so you can stop worrying now and concentrate on the job we came here to do. This is a brillfanmagical place to reduce the odds from, so let's do it. Let's pelt them with balloon bombs and water bottles, and see how much they don't like them.'

So they started dropping and slinging the bombs.

David's first milk bomb missed the head of the one he was aiming for, but when it burst it splashed the legs of two other Roundheads. They tried to escape the bombardment by running away but failed miserably as their legs dissolved under them and they too became bubbling heaps of mucus sludge and uniforms.

David's parents had a little more luck with their first attempts, not only did their milk bombs score bulls-eyes, but they both took out the ones on either side of their main targets with the splashes. The gooey mess they made when they all finally disintegrated was awful. That left only the two entities being toyed with by Sir Gawain.

'Let's all go down and finish them off,' David said, 'that will leave only Offalmire to deal with.' And taking a firm grip of his parents' hands, he flew them down with him from the top of the King's Tower, his dad still tightly clutching their black carry-all bag containing, amongst other things, their so very important 'P' jar.

'Have a rest for a minute, Sir Gawain,' Sylvia said with a smile, 'but disarm them first please.'

Sir Gawain smiled back, nodded and then with a few deft flicks of his sword, relieved both goblin Roundheads of the fearsome weapons they had, and stepped well back. A physical fight then began similar to the one which had taken place on Tollvale beach.

There was nothing the Knight family enjoyed more than a proper bout of unarmed combat, and Sylvia felt as though she needed to get her own back a bit as she had been the one who had been attacked and tied up on the beach.

Their opponents turned out to be better fighters than swordsmen. Magically, they were very cleverly copying Bill and Sylvia's moves and what originally seemed a push-over began to develop into something very different. Sadly, because Offalmire was now also supernaturally assisting them, his men were magically becoming stronger and David could also see his parents were at the same time magically being drained of energy. They were in trouble. If the now one-sided scrap was allowed to continue it could only get worse.

'Offalmire is cheating! He is manipulating the fight so you both can be killed!' David angrily shouted. 'I'm going to put a stop to it, and now.' He then took his water pistol from his belt and squirted it into the faces of his parents' sickly grinning opponents, who wrongly thought they were about to win. Their expressions soon changed, and they made the same strange whining noises the others had made as they made vain attempts to back away from what had been splashed on to them. But they too dissolved into the usual mucus sludge.

The area was now littered with assorted dropped weapons and slimey mucus soaked uniform piles. It really was beginning to look like a sort of very messy battlefield.

'Thanks for that, Son, that was the last of them,' Bill said, 'thirteen I counted.' And they all picked up a sword as possible souvenirs or in case Offalmire became violent when they went to rescue Mary.

However, their plans were suddenly and dramatically changed; totally quashed in fact. For as they walked round the King's Tower to where King Offalmire was holding Mary, they were confronted by yet another new line of thirteen more sinister and threatening looking goblin Roundheads that Offalmire had somehow cloned. They were standing between them and Offalmire and Bill couldn't help blurting out, 'Aw shit!'

Then the air, buildings, walls and even the ground beneath their feet trembled as Offalmire angrily bellowed out: 'YOU ARE THE SCUM OF THE EARTH. YOU AND OTHERS LIKE YOU, MEDDLING WITH THINGS YOU DON'T UNDERSTAND. I MAY BE SMALLER NOW, BUT I AM FAR FROM BEING FINISHED.'

Then looking down at Mary he continued, 'I HAVE YOUR DAUGHTER AND I KNOW SHE IS A KEY. I WILL USE HER TO GET ME INTO THE CRYSTAL TOWER. I CAN THEN EAT HER.'

And he commanded his soldiers to attack.

David grabbed the large water cannon from the bag his dad was carrying and on this occasion his first shot was deadly accurate, drenching the nearest three Roundheads. As always, the cow's milk's effects were devastatingly good, resulting in three more sickly piles of snot soaked uniforms. The next three soldiers, having seen what was happening, faltered, that is until Offalmire bellowed at them, scaring them even more. They too then went the same way as the others. Seven were left, but David's cannon was now empty.

A big groan then came from everyone as yet another thirteen Roundheads suddenly appeared and Offalmire simply roared with laughter, which didn't help.

But unknown to their parents, and it took them completely by surprise, David and Mary had cunningly prepared a back-up plan, and it was now time to use it. Looking up into the sky, David shouted, 'NOW WOULD BE A GOOD TIME 'RED' AND MABEL, WHEN YOU'RE READY!'

His remarks brought a brief pause in the action that had just started and everyone looked up as unbelievably a red dragon materialized in the sky above them. It was Red, their friendly dragon, and he was not alone. Suspended beneath him was Mabel the black and white cow and she had a small sledge type platform slung under her belly.

Shouting his thanks, David flew up to position himself face down on the sledge but in a way which allowed him to be able to reach Mabel's udder.

'READY WHEN YOU ARE!' David shouted. Red then did a fantastic job, repeatedly making runs over the heads of the soldiers while David expertly squeezing Mabel's teats showered milk on to all of Offalmire's now screaming and writhing Roundheads. Red's flapping wings also created air turbulence that helped distribute the falling milk even more effectively.

With Sir Gawain's expert swordsmanship and his skill with a knife, and with the twins' parents fighting skills added to Red's, Mabel's and David's superb efforts, the battle that seemed almost endless, was won.

The whole area was by now looking very untidy. There was a gooey snotty mess littered with mucus-drenched piles of uniforms everywhere and a few motionless Roundhead bodies. Redundant swords and knives were scattered all over the area, some sticking up in the air.

Offalmire had somehow managed to amble and shuffle close to the ground floor door of the King's Tower while the fighting was in progress and now looked out of breath and totally dejected. His disgusting breath from his heavy breathing, coupled with a release of more body gas, became a big mistake.

Mary, having been held close to his slimy, repulsive side for so long, her stomach continually wretching as his foul smells continued assaulting her nose, was now, not surprisingly, feeling very ill. And finally, as some of his snot dripped off his chest onto her arm, she could stand it no more and was violently sick. She threw up down Offamire's leg and across his feet.

At first he laughed as he thought it was very funny, but his smile was short-lived for what had erupted from Mary's very upset stomach was now burning into his leg and feet. This made him take a staggering step backwards and he fortunately released his grip on Mary who immediately took advantage of it and stepped a few paces away from his now trembling and swaying obnoxious body.

Slipping her hand into her rucksack she pulled out two of their special water bottle bombs and hurled them at the side of the King's Tower where they instantly shattered, showering their contents over Offalmire. She also sprayed some cream at his face which fell round his mouth and chin, making him look like the most unlikely Father Christmas you are ever likely to see.

Then, as Mary's parents had observed what she had done, they did the same, smashing more bottles above Offalmire.

Having been the recipient of more Knights' water showers, which were definitely having an effect, the obnoxious King Offalmire no longer looked so threatening. In fact, he looked positively humble and extremely unhappy.

He was still trying to bellow and roar, but miserably failing, as his body like those of the other goblins before him, slowly began to quiver and bubble as it steadily melted down. It was however, a much slower process because of his supernatural powers, which were all gradually failing.

Also, sadly for him, as his feet and legs got worse and David laughingly said, 'That's rotted his socks off good and proper,' Offalmire lost his balance and flopped down. Unfortunately for him, as he flopped down backwards he landed on a sword that was pointing upwards, and that did make him scream. Then, screaming and with his mouth wide open, he helplessly dropped on his back.

David, had just landed on the King's Tower with Red and Mabel, and seeing Offalmire lying on his back with his mouth wide open, just couldn't resist the opportunity. He carefully and very deliberately dropped his last milk bomb straight down and into it, his dad expertly throwing a fork to burst it just as it went in. At this point Sir Gawain fitted the poisoned arrow into the special yew bow and took careful aim as Offalmire struggled up to a seated position.

Unfortunately, neither Sir Gawain nor any of the others had noticed that one of the Roundheads, who seemingly had been lying still, only wounded and not dead, had picked up a sword. Before anyone could stop him and with a powerful swirling blow, he chopped the arrow and bow being held by Sir Gawain completely in two...

Both Sylvia and Mary then simultaneously experienced problems, their hands on their mouths failing to stifle their screams of, 'NO...O! NO...O...O!

Offalmire, though in trouble and now desperately trying to remain upright, had seen everything and hoarsely shouted: 'THE MILK AND YOUR WATER WILL HURT FOR A LITTLE WHILE, BUT MY POWERS CAN AND WILL REPAIR MY BODY. I WILL THEN BE EVEN STRONGER AND WILL BE ABLE TO ENTER THE CRYSTAL TOWER WITHOUT YOUR DAUGHTER'S HELP.'

Mary had run to join her parents while Offalmire had been spouting and they both tightly hugged her.

Offalmire, having now painfully succeeded in managing to prop himself up with his long arms, continued with his ranting, but having lost the ability to shout was now only able to speak in a much quieter croaky voice. 'You, the Terrestrial Twins and your family and supporters were not clever enough, strong enough or wise enough to beat me, King Offalmire. I have won this battle because you can no longer kill me…You no longer have a killing arrow or bow.'

'NO, THEY HAVEN'T, BUT I MOST CERTAINLY HAVE!' shouted an archer dressed in a Lincoln green tunic and cap, brown tights and brown boots and who had suddenly materialized as Offalmire started trying to shout. Before materializing, he had invisibly removed the 'P' jar from Bill's bag and dipped two more special yew tree arrows in the poison potion ready for action.

He wasted no time at all, and within seconds of appearing his first special yew tree arrow streaked across the lawn and bedded itself in King Offalmire's left eye. Then, even though Offalmire was reeling about like a demented animal, first screaming like a pig and then bellowing like a bull, a second arrow found its target in his right eye. At the same moment as the twins had called upon the Gods of the Terrestrial Light for their part in the occasion, Offalmire's sorry looking body was engulfed in a brilliant beam of bright white and blue almost blinding, shimmering light.

The mixed collection of observers then stood quietly together to thankfully observe King Offalmire's last moments. The unusual group consisted of the black and white haired Terrestrial Twins with their black and white haired parents who were standing next to an Arthurian Knight in black and white armour. He was standing next to a black and white cow and next to her, and who's presence was a big surprise to some, stood Robin Hood. And the whole friendly and powerful group was standing in the shadow of a magnificent red dragon.

They all watched as King Offalmire, the evil leader of the Other World, was removed from theirs. After parting with his last burp and fart, his body was finally reduced to no more than a repulsive pile of muddy, bubbling, runny mucus. The beam of light then faded. It was finally all over. The fight of good over evil had been won. Thankfully King Offalmire was at last dead.

'Using Red and Mabel was a brilliant idea, kids,' Bill said as they walked a few paces from the battlefield, 'it was a stroke of pure genius.'

'I liked it when…That was Robin Hood, wasn't it?'

The twins were both smiling as they nodded yes, to their mum. 'When he arrived and shot those two arrows, that was the best bit for me. That was very clever planning. Well done, kids.'

'We had asked Sir Gawain to make two bows and four arrows as well as choosing a supporting archer,' Mary said, 'and let's face it, he did an excellent job. But I think we all did.'

They thanked Sir Gawain and Robin Hood for all they had done and the pair of them together said, 'Our pleasure,' smiled, nodded and faded away.

Red then said Mabel had gone back for milking but doubted she'd have much to give. He said how much he had enjoyed all the experiences and for his name and hoped they'd invite him to the next event, if there ever was to be one, and then he disappeared.

'That's it,' David said, 'we've achieved our objective.'

'Yes,' Mary agreed, 'we won. Offalmire is no more.'

'And the Thirteen Treasures are still safe too,' Bill proudly said, 'you twins have done a brilliant job.'

'Yes, well done all of you,' Merlin said, having just appeared behind them. 'You have all done a real service to humanity and I am proud to have been associated with you. All of you! He then surprised them when he waved his hands over where the action had been and said, 'Battlefield, tidy.' There was a quick flash of pale blue shimmering light and the grass was perfectly clean again, other than one faintly lighter and wet mark where King Offalmire's remains had been.

'You will find your cutlery in the bottom of your bag when you get back to your cottage,' he said. Then he went on to say, 'On behalf of the Gods of the Terrestrial Light, I wish to thank you, the Terrestrial Twins, for doing such a complete job. Your destiny itself is now complete. I trust you will find and make good use of your newly acquired powers and abilities.'

'Won't they go away now?' Sylvia asked in an apprehensive voice, 'after we've left Castershire.'

'No,' replied Merlin, 'they will be with you for the rest of your lives. They also will grow stronger and more comprehensive, and will be passed to your children in one form or another. You have to make sure you never misuse them. It's more than likely I may wish to call upon your developing special powers in the future. Time will tell. Enjoy the rest of your holiday!'

Then he was gone.

The twins looked like they had just taken some nasty tasting medicine. They were speechless. In fact they all were.

'Be with us for the rest of our lives. Passed to our children!' David pronounced in a shocked voice. 'Brillfanmagical! I think!'

Mary, also looking shocked, simply said, 'Me too!'

Their mum held a hand of each of her twins and quietly said, 'You'll both be all right, you'll see. You'll soon get used to your *whatever it is* you now have.' Everyone laughed!

Bill had just suggested they call on Red for a final word on the way out when David managed to get in the last word. 'I know Offalmire said we were sticking our noses in where they weren't wanted, but I'm glad in the end he saw the point that Sir Gawain had made, not only once, but twice!' And his last comment brought a smile to all their faces.

As they reached the entrance to the King's Banqueting Hall for a chat with Red, the seven magpies appeared.

'We really enjoyed being able to help,' their leader said, 'who knows, we may be seeing all of you again. There may be more stories just waiting to be told...'

"MYSTICAL MAGPIES & MYTHOLOGY"

A SERIES OF FOUR SEQUENTIAL STORIES
by
ALAN PRINCIPAL

Four 'crossover' captivating action packed and magical
adventures. Exciting family reading suitable for the 'young
at heart' from 10 to 100.

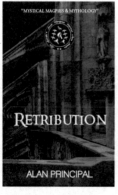

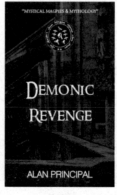

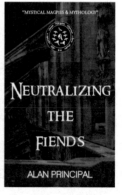